"Frederick…Lord Surd?"

He raised up to gaze intently into the depths of her brilliant green eyes. "Yes, Miss Collins?"

"I wished to mention…" She paused. "While I do not anticipate requiring help, thank you for your offer. I feel comforted knowing you are close by."

He smiled as he made a deliberate, gradual movement, inconspicuously caressing her fingers before releasing her hand. "Your words bring me great assurance. It is my sincere hope my presence will always be a source of pleasure to you."

Praise for Cynthia Moore

Better Than a Present

"A Fun and Entertaining Short Story."

~ My Book Addiction

"The characters are pleasant, and the story is well written. The author has a good feel for the time period and its customs."

~ Coffee Time Romance

I Wish for Your Kiss

"Good Reading"

~ LAS Review

Bewildered in Bath

by

Cynthia Moore

Road To Romance, Book 3

Bewildered in Bath

Cover Art by *Tina Lynn Stout*

The Wild Rose Press, Inc.
PO Box 708
Adams Basin, NY 14410-0708
Visit us at www.thewildrosepress.com

Publishing History
First Edition, 2023
Trade Paperback ISBN 978-1-5092-4856-8
Digital ISBN 978-1-5092-4857-5

Road To Romance, Book 3
Published in the United States of America

Dedication

To Darlene and Randy with happy memories of our trips to Bath.

Chapter One

Hyde Park, London, late September 1819

"We intend to leave by nine o'clock Monday morning," Miss Camille Collins reminded her friend, Miss Ellen Cather.

"I will be ready," Miss Cather promised as she walked away, closely trailed by her maid.

"Camille? Miss Collins?"

She turned around. "Good day, Lord Surd!"

"I did not expect to find you here in London. When did you arrive?"

She hadn't seen Frederick for several weeks. Camille studied him before replying. His thick yellow-gold hair was combed back off a high forehead to fall in soft waves at the back of his neck, just above his collar. His wide brown eyes were framed by curved, thin brows. His slender nose had a hint of a classic aristocratic bend at the tip, and a firm chin extended beneath his full lips. "Mother and I have been in the city for three days. We leave for Bath the day after tomorrow."

His brows rose. "I believe Bath is at its best during the spring and summer. Do you and Lady Collins expect to take a short excursion there?"

"Not at all!" She looked over her shoulder to check on the location of her maid. She stood a few yards away, feeding some ducks bits of stale bread. Camille lowered her voice. "Were you aware Edward recently married Lady Sophia?"

His mouth cleaved open. "Ahem! Your brother and Lady Sophia! You astonish me!"

Camille smiled at his reaction. "We were surprised by the news as well. They were married a week ago by special license. Mother had planned to pay a visit to a widowed childhood friend who lives in Bath next spring. She felt it prudent to take the journey now so that Edward and Sophia may begin their lives together without undue interference. Of course, I agreed to accompany her. Miss Cather comes with us as well."

He frowned. "How long does your mother plan to visit?"

"Nothing is certain. She advised me she believes we will be there at least two months."

"That long? Where will you be staying?"

"Because the city is less crowded this time of year, we were fortunate to obtain a townhouse in the Royal Crescent." She paused, to gaze intently at him. "Why are you quizzing me in such a resolute manner?"

"Forgive me!" He reached for her hand, his cheeks flushed, his brown eyes gleaming. "You cannot be surprised...you must understand. Camille, Miss Collins, I had intended to visit your brother at Horsham House next week and formally apply for permission to pay my addresses to you."

Her heart began to race, the frantic beats reverberating loudly in her ears. She stared at him, unable to speak. Her mouth flapped open and shut like a fish out of water, suddenly finding itself tossed upon a sandy shore. She cleared her throat and took a deep breath.

"I am honored to have received such exemplary notice from you, my lord. However, I am not ready to settle down. I have many things to accomplish before I think of marriage." Out of the corner of her eye, Camille saw her maid walking toward her. "I must go."

****

Frederick opened the study door, striding inside to make his way to the drink's table. He poured a large quantity of brandy into a glass. After taking a swift gulp, he walked across the room to sit in his father's favorite chair. Reclining back against the soft cushions, he frowned up at the coffered ceiling. After her initial dumbfounded reaction, there had not been much opportunity for Camille to provide him with a comprehensive reply to his declaration. *Had he misunderstood her depth of feeling for him?* The first time he had seen Camille, he was twenty-one and had just returned to London after completing his studies at Cambridge.

He woke up early that morning to bright sunlight and the soothing sounds of bird songs from the trees outside his window. The day was too lovely to waste a moment more lying in his bed. He dressed himself in his riding clothes and walked to the nearby mews to retrieve his horse. Enjoying the crisp, early morning air and the sensation of being alone in a normally crowded locality, he spurred his horse to a canter, soon arriving at Hyde Park. He remembered experiencing a pang of disappointment when he spied a young girl accompanied by a groom riding together a short distance away. He studied her awkward seat on the animal, quickly determining she was learning how to ride, and he pulled back on the reins, resolving to lead his horse away from them to the other side of the park.

At that moment, a rabbit darted out from a nearby bush, startling the mare. The horse reared, causing the reins to drop from the girl's hands. She screamed, clutching the side saddle with tense fingers. Before the groom could reach her side, Frederick spurred his horse forward to swing out and grab the dangling reins. Using a combination of soothing words and brute strength, he gradually calmed the mare down. When the horse came to a complete stop, the girl released her grip on the saddle and wrapped her arms around his neck. She kissed his cheek with a loud smack before exclaiming, "You saved me!"

From that moment, five years ago, Frederick had been her devoted, steadfast admirer. With maturity and shared, memorable experiences, his feelings for her gradually deepened into love.

He took another sip of brandy and heard someone clear their throat. The butler stood in the doorway. "Yes, Quentin?"

"My lord, Mr. Rudder is inquiring if you are at home."

He rose from the chair, placing his glass on a nearby table. "Yes. Please send him in."

Moments later, his friend strolled into the room, stopping on the threshold to execute a bow. "Hallo, Frederick. Good of you to see me."

"Of course. You are always welcome, John. Come in and sit down. Would you care for brandy? I was just having some."

"Yes. I will join you." He settled himself in the chair on the other side of the table. "Rather early in the day for you, isn't it? Are you celebrating something?"

Frederick poured the amber liquid into a glass and handed it to him. He sat down once more, favoring his companion with a direct, unwavering gaze. He met John the previous summer, at an informal party in the countryside given by Camille's mother, Lady Collins. An honorable, pleasant gentleman, son of Viscount Tilbrook, he was a favorite with young, unmarried ladies because of his height, muscular frame, and ruggedly handsome countenance. To Frederick's knowledge, John remained unattached. During the visit at the Collins' estate, there had been opportunity to have numerous discussions together covering a variety of topics. Frederick discovered they shared compatible, harmonious views on even the most ponderous of subjects. A chance meeting had developed into a firm friendship. "As a matter of fact, I mean to drown my sorrows."

"As bad as that? What has happened?"

He cleared his throat. "I planned to travel to Horsham next week to ask Sir Edward for permission to court his sister."

"Congratulations! It is about time, old man," his friend teased. "However, I doubt if you will find Sir Edward at home. You do understand he got married a few days ago?"

"Yes. I had no idea the event was generally known."

"I have knowledge of it because I was one of the wedding party," John countered with a grin.

Frederick sat up straight in his chair. "You were there?"

"Sir Edward asked me to serve as a witness at the ceremony. Although I was not provided with many details, I believe their decision to marry was done in haste." He frowned. "I am certain they will not be away for too many days, a fortnight at the most. He undoubtedly has many responsibilities to oversee on his estate. Surely such a minimal delay to make your request to Sir Edward would be no cause for sorrow?"

Frederick winced. "Of course not. A slight postponement would not dim my feelings of joy had my intended bride welcomed my proposal."

"Miss Collins spurned your offer? I don't understand. As a matter of fact, I am dumbfounded!"

"I am astonished as well."

John took a sip of his brandy. "I have observed the two of you together on many occasions. There was no doubt in my mind you were both equally captivated with each other. This is quite puzzling. Did she give you a reason for her refusal?"

"There wasn't much time for her to explain," Frederick clarified with a frown. "I hadn't meant to blurt out my intentions to her in such a crass manner. I came upon Miss Collins by chance in Hyde Park. She first inquired if I had knowledge of her brother's recent marriage and informed me of her plans to accompany her mother to visit a friend in Bath to allow the newly wedded couple some privacy. I asked how long she would be away and where she was staying. She became confused by my barrage of questions and asked for an explanation."

"I can't say I blame the lady."

"I had the entire event orchestrated in my head and no suspicion of anything out of the ordinary occurring to make my plans go awry," he retorted with a sigh. "I informed Miss Collins of my intention to approach Sir Edward for his consent, and she became as nervous as a newborn colt. She babbled a few sentences, mentioning her appreciation for my regard, indicating she was not ready to settle down, there were many things to be accomplished first, and so on, before her maid joined her. She murmured a hasty farewell to me and quit the park. All my careful plans splintered into a disheveled heap at my feet."

"I am sorry to hear this. Do you have a notion how you will proceed?"

"My first thought was to follow her to Bath and continue to plead my case. After deliberating the matter, I am hesitant to advance upon her with such a bold, headstrong aspect. You are acquainted with Miss Collins. It would never do to conduct myself with a cloying, grasping demeanor in her presence."

"No, never that! At the same time, you must endeavor to keep yourself within her inner circle of friends," John advised. "I suggest you go to Bath and adopt the role of impromptu attendant. Do not hover over her but allow her to understand you intend to be her defender should she ever require assistance."

Frederick pondered his proposition. "Yes! I believe you have stumbled upon a capital concept. My continued presence in her immediate vicinity will insure I am not consigned to oblivion while she procures new acquaintances in Bath. An additional compensation is the ability to come to her rescue if the situation warrants it."

"Just what is needed! You will be her gallant champion. She will soon fall into your arms declaring her love for you!"

He raised his brows, imagining the wonderful sensation of clasping Camille to his chest. "I hesitate to validate the romantic vision you have conjured up, but I would certainly welcome such a display of affection from her. Thank you very much for your sage advice."

"A pleasure."

Frederick frowned as his thoughts reverted to the present. "I apologize. You came to see me. Is there something you require?"

John chuckled. "It is nothing as important as your dilemma. I planned to ask if you would join me for dinner at White's this evening."

"I would be happy to." He paused, hearing a knock on the door. "Come in."

His father, the Earl of Gladden stood on the threshold and sketched a bow. "Frederick, Mr. Rudder. I am sorry to interrupt. This won't take long. I wanted to inform you, Frederick, I received a letter from your uncle. He is suffering from a rather severe run of gout and has gone to stay in Bath for a few weeks to take the waters. He asks if you could visit him there."

Frederick glanced at John. He noted his friend's smug expression as he struggled to hold back the laughter that threatened to erupt from his mouth. "There is nothing I would like better, Father!"

Chapter Two

Camille stared out of the coach window, contemplating the passing scenery without seeing it. She had yet to recover her composure since Lord Surd divulged his intention to pay his addresses to her.

Her mother sighed. "I had forgotten how tedious it is to travel on the Bath Road. At least it is not raining."

"It has been some time since we stopped at the Maidenhead tollgate," pointed out Ellen from her seat on the opposite side of the carriage. "It shouldn't be too long before we arrive in Reading."

"You are remarkably familiar with the territory, my dear," Lady Margaret Collins commented with raised brows.

Ellen's cheeks flushed. "My cousins Abigail, Thomas, and I have always been close. They reside in Bristol with my aunt. I have frequently traveled this road with my parents to visit them."

"I had forgotten you had family in Bristol," Lady Collins remarked. "Camille, you have barely spoken the entire journey. It is not like you. Are you ill?"

She roused herself, turning from the window. "I apologize, Mother. I am tired. I did not sleep well last night."

"You were awake early this morning preparing to travel as well." Ellen smiled at her.

"Yes, that is true." She cleared her throat. "Are we

stopping for tea soon, Mother?"

"Yes. We change horses at Reading," she informed her. "I have arranged for a light respite to be served in a private parlor at The George. We will spend the night at the Castle Inn in Marlborough and should arrive in Bath late in the afternoon on Wednesday."

"Oh, lovely!" gushed Ellen. "I have never been inside the inn. I understand the interiors are quite fine."

"I stopped there many years ago with my husband shortly after we were married. It was originally home to the Duke of Somerset," Lady Collins explained, turning to her daughter. "You will find much to interest you, Camille. The furnishings are exquisite. Some pieces date back to the sixteenth century."

She forced her lips to move into a semblance of a smile. "I look forward to it."

Her mother studied her for several moments. "Would you have preferred to stay in London? I realize your first season was cut short when we were summoned to Berkshire to check on your brother after he was injured falling off his horse."

"No. Not at all, Mother," she assured her. "While I am happy to have attended the myriad of parties, balls, and social gatherings, it was not an experience I am eager to continue. Perhaps because we spent so much time in London before I had my formal come out, I admit the whirlwind of activities hold little appeal."

"Bath is known for its stunning architecture. Many of the buildings are covered in delicate golden limestone. It also has a much slower, less frantic social setting," Ellen pointed out.

"You are correct." Her mother reached out to pat Camille's hand. "Perhaps you will find the moderate pace in the city more to your liking."

"I understand one must take a chair or walk to get around the foremost districts of Bath because of the steep inclines and the narrow streets," she commented, not wanting her distraction to spoil the journey for the others. "Is this true?"

"Yes, it is. Carriages are generally driven only in the outskirts of town. The slopes and hills, as well as the narrow streets that cover the central quarter of the city, are unsuitable for most vehicles," Lady Collins clarified, as the coach rolled to a stop. "It appears we have arrived in Reading. I will check to see if the parlor is ready for our use. Our maids and grooms should be right behind us."

They emerged from their carriage to find Sally and her mother's maid Maud, waiting for them. Lady Collins led the way to the front of the inn, with Camille and Ellen following behind. They stepped inside the elegant, marble titled entry.

"Welcome, my lady." The innkeeper bowed to Lady Collins. "I trust you had a pleasant journey from London?"

"We have, sir," she answered him with a sigh. "It is good to be out of the confining space for a short time. I arranged for tea in a private parlor?"

"Yes, my lady, through here." He indicated a door on his right as a short, rosy cheeked lady in a frilly lace cap joined him. "The fire has been built up. The room is quite comfortable. We will serve you whenever you are ready. My wife will conduct you to the retiring room."

"Thank you." She turned around. "Ladies, bring Sally with you. I wish to take a short stroll outside with Maud."

"Very well, Mother." Camille followed the innkeeper's wife down a long passage adorned with several portraits of fashionable people amusing themselves in various lush, green gardens. The woman stopped near the end of the corridor and motioned them to follow her to a recess under the stairway to a door tucked back in the corner. She opened it with a flourish.

"There is fresh water and towels, the commode is behind the screen, and a dressing table with a mirror for your convenience," she announced. "Your tea will be waiting in the parlor."

"Thank you." Camille entered first with the other two women following close behind.

"I would not have believed such a large room could be fitted underneath a stairway," commented Ellen.

"Perhaps this was the housekeeper's quarters before it became an inn, Miss?" queried Sally.

"You are likely correct," Camille observed. "Several of the buildings were originally private homes. Recall, Mother informed us the Duke of Somerset once resided at The Castle Inn, the place where we are staying tonight. Sally, would you comb out my hair and refasten it?"

"Yes, of course, Miss Collins."

"Excuse me." Ellen disappeared behind the screen.

Camille sat down at the dressing table and stared in the mirror as the maid took the pins from her hair. She studied her reflection. Her dark brown hair fell in thick, curly strands to a point just above her waist. She preferred to wear it gathered into a cluster of small loops on the crown of her head, often encircled by an elegant head piece. Parted in the middle, jaunty ebony- brown ringlets clustered and framed her face. Thin, dusky eyebrows hovered over what she believed was her best feature, her emerald-green eyes. The color often varied to match her emotions. She had been told they turned grey and stormy as seafoam when she was angry or brilliant as a leafy fern when something amusing made her laugh.

She frowned at her button nose, small mouth, and pert red lips, thinking them features from her childhood that had not matured with the rest of her body. Her soft, rounded cheeks and tiny, shell-like ears completed her attributes.

Frederick's, Lord Surd's, bewildering pronouncement once again surfaced into her disordered thoughts. His hasty declaration forced her to examine her feelings for him. What were they? She admitted to herself she took for granted he would always come to her aid if she required his assistance. Were those sensations a natural condition resulting from their first meeting, saving her from falling off her horse when she was fourteen years old? Or was it a result of years of close friendship that, unbeknownst to her, had grown into the deeper emotion of love?

"You are finished, Miss Collins," Sally's strident voice broke into her thoughts. "Miss Cather, would you like your hair brushed out as well?"

Camille blinked, attempting to concentrate on the present, and stood up from the dressing table. She and Ellen had agreed to share her lady's maid while staying in Bath for purposes of efficiency. The probable, insignificant number of events they would attend in the city would not require the assistance of two maids. "I imagine our tea will be ready soon."

"I believe my hair does require some attention."

Ellen moved across the room from her position by the window. "I wonder if there will be many other young ladies as well as eligible gentlemen residing in Bath this time of year? It would be quite agreeable to gain new acquaintances, don't you agree, Camille?"

Ellen's query dislodged a recollection from the past, the summer house party at her brother's country estate last year, given just before she turned eighteen. Her mother had styled the event as an informal way for Camille to meet a few young men before the stringent ritual of her first season in London. Lord Surd had attended as well. She recalled her sense of relief when he arrived. The other gentlemen were amiable and often diverting, but nothing could compare to her feelings of affinity and the sense of security she experienced when Frederick stood by her side. How was she to proceed without his comforting presence over the next several weeks?

Chapter Three

Frederick rapped on the door at the address his uncle had given him on Alfred Street. The threshold was partially covered by an arched pediment. From the outside, the townhouse appeared to be of excellent construction. Eight twelve pane windows glimmered in the late afternoon light from the three-story structure. Two elongated chimneys emerged from a pitched, shallow roof.

The door opened just as he raised his hand to knock a second time.

"Good afternoon, my lord!"

"Rigsby! Is my uncle at home?"

"Yes, he is here."

"Excellent! I left my horses and carriage at the stable off Bennett Street. My valet will be here shortly with my luggage."

"Very good, my lord. Would you wish me to take you to Mr. Melter now?"

"Please. I will greet him while I wait for a change of clothes to arrive."

"Follow me."

Frederick trailed the butler from the main entry, and then along a compact passage. A staircase appeared in front of them. Rigsby turned to the left, continuing down another corridor, before opening the door a few paces away.

"Lord Surd to see you, Mr. Melter."

Frederick strode inside the room to spy his uncle sitting in a chair placed directly in front of the hearth. One of his feet was propped up on a stool.

"Come in, come in, Frederick! You made good time. Sorry I can't get up and greet you properly. This blasted gout!"

He studied the man in front him, noticing for the first time the similarities in their appearance. His uncle had the same yellow, gold-colored hair and deep brown eyes as he did. His father's hair was a dark brown and his eyes were a combination of green and brown. "Wonderful to see you, sir. How are you feeling?"

He grimaced. "I knew I'd pay a price for drinking too much brandy and eating sumptuous foods, but I had no notion it would be this painful."

"I am grieved to hear you are in so much distress," he sympathized, sitting in a chair across from him. "Does drinking the waters help at all?"

"Humph!" The older gentleman wrinkled his nose. "The water gives me a belly ache whenever I swallow the abominable stuff. I have soaked in the spa on a few occasions. It served to relieve some of the discomfort."

"Well, that is something," he remarked with fortitude. "Is there anything in particular you would like me to help you with?"

"Just keep an uncomfortable, lonely man company for a while, if you please, Frederick." He sighed. "I don't expect you to constantly be at my beck and call. As you noted, I brought Rigsby with me as well as a couple of footmen, and Mrs. Rigsby, my cook. My valet, Gimble will take care of the usual personal necessities. I would like you to accompany me to the Pump Room occasionally in the afternoons, perhaps take a sip of the ghastly water, join me for a soak in the King's Spa, play a few rounds of chess after dinner in the evenings, that sort of thing."

"I will gladly perform those tasks, sir."

"The winter bathing season runs through the end of September until the end of March," his uncle continued. "I understand the formal season begins the first of October and continues until Christmas. I expect you to attend the concerts and balls held in the Assembly Rooms. The Upper Rooms are but a short walk from here. Don't hole yourself up here with me day and night!"

"Very well. If that is your wish," he countered, experiencing a sense of relief, mixed with guilt, as he realized he had been contemplating how best to abandon his uncle in order to spend some time with Miss Collins.

"I never leave my bedchamber before eleven when I break my fast," his uncle clarified. "I prefer to read for a time after I wake up. You are free to do as you like in the mornings."

"You are quite gracious, sir," he told him with sincerity. "I do intend to make your well-being my top priority no matter how hard you try to force me to seek entertainment elsewhere!"

He chuckled. "I admire your intentions, but you are a young, handsome gentleman. You must mingle with the ladies. There will not be the crowds you are used to in London, but I glimpsed several lovely young women in the Pump Room a few days ago."

Frederick realized his uncle had never had occasion to meet Camille. He was a confirmed bachelor who rarely left his estate near Reading. "May I ask why you never married?"

He sighed. "I believe you could say it was mostly for selfish reasons."

"Selfish, sir?"

"I was twenty-three years old and your father thirty, when he met your mother and fell in love. They married, you were born within a year, and he had his heir. A few years later, I decided to visit London. My small estate had an efficient steward making certain all ran smoothly without my constant presence. I was then twenty-six, a prosperous, upstanding landowner and considered a 'catch'." He reached down to rub his knee with a scowl on his face. "I joined a group of young sons of wealthy peers. They all had access to large sums of money and were bored with their lives of leisure, a dangerous combination. I gambled and visited brothels with them, caroused and drank until the early morning hours. I was seduced by what first appeared to be a carefree existence, but I soon became aware of a nagging sense of guilt and shame. One night, I sobered up enough to eschew the gaming establishments and attend a ball."

Frederick tried and failed to picture his honorable uncle in such a pernicious, disheartened condition. "What happened?"

He stared at the fireplace for several seconds without speaking. "I fell in love."

"In love? So quickly?"

"I suppose others would argue it was nothing more than a passing attraction. After all, how could it be possible to know in a matter of seconds that another person completes you?" He took a deep breath before continuing, "We danced a cotillion; you know how frustrating that situation can be. The opportunity for any sort of conversation is minimal. Over the next hour, I never lost sight of her. At the end of a particularly strident reel, I heard her decline other invitations to dance, instead stating her intention to sit down and catch her breath. I seized the opportunity and took the chair next to her."

"Certainly, a most opportune occurrence," Frederick remarked, with a grin.

"She turned and spoke to me. I will never forget her words."

"I am surprised to see you here. How did you get inside?"

"I received an invitation. Pardon me, have we been introduced?"

"No, not formally. It was impossible for me to avoid encountering you when you landed in a drunken heap at my feet during the ball celebrating my betrothal a week ago."

"I remember the sensation of the blood draining from my face when I understood she was to be married. I struggled to form words to reply to her. "I…I attended your…your ball?"

"The correct phrase would be, 'you made an appearance'. Thankfully, the debacle happened shortly after you and the others snuck inside. Your friends picked you up off the floor and carried you away."

"You can understand why I immediately got up from the chair and left without explaining my feelings. She would have been insulted and certainly laughed in my face. I summoned what little remained of my dignity, took my leave of her, and departed London early the next morning. I have never forgotten her or stopped blaming myself for my actions. If I hadn't been so self-indulgent and completely consumed with participating in all types of indecorous revelry, I might have met her in more promising circumstances. Perhaps even before she was betrothed."

Frederick cleared his throat, resisting the urge to fidget when the sobering thought of losing Camille to another man burst into his consciousness. "I am sorry to hear of this. Most of the young gentlemen I am acquainted with have been castaway or under the hatches after a night of rollicking in London. I have had my share of bosky evenings when I threw away disconcerting amounts of money on gaming, only to wake up the next morning with a headache and a feeling of great remorse. Did you ever learn the lady's name? Have you encountered her since that day?"

"No," he uttered the word in a bleak tone. "I suffered much anguish when I returned to my estate. I replayed the various escapades I had participated in, the ones I could recall, over and over in my head. My actions were shameful. I couldn't stomach the thought of approaching her and seeing an expression of disgust on her face."

"That would certainly be awkward," he agreed. "I believe you are too hard on yourself, sir. I doubt she felt repulsion for you. Rather, I imagine she was diverted by the situation. After all, as I pointed out, one encounters drunken young men quite often during the season."

"I appreciate your attempt to make light of my disgrace, Frederick. Thankfully, one rarely confronts befuddled simpletons at a ball celebrating one's upcoming marriage! I behaved like a frivolous, cabbage-headed blade!" He gestured to his elevated leg. "I suppose this is a just and fitting punishment."

"The discomfort you are experiencing at present is

not a reparation, Uncle. You admitted you overindulged on food and drink. The gout is a consequence of that. I understand your heart belongs to another and you feel you will never be able to love again, but perhaps you could meet a lady who would be a comfortable friend. Someone it would be possible for you to grow to care for and enjoy being in her company?"

His uncle turned away to stare at something across the room and sighed. "Until lately, when I was forced to sit and do nothing but ruminate about my life, I hadn't a notion I pined for female companionship. I managed to keep quite busy with day-to-day tasks involved in managing my estate. My recent reflections on possible explanations for my actions have led me to grudgingly acknowledge I purposely avoided facing my loneliness by giving myself no opportunity to deliberate on the circumstance."

"Do you plan on returning to London to seek an introduction to someone acceptable to you?" Frederick inquired.

His uncle twisted around on the chair to look at him. "I can't endeavor to woo any lady until I am able to walk again. The thought of rejoining the wild fray in the metropolis makes me shudder, although at my age I certainly wouldn't be accompanying the pretentious rakes looking over the young women offered on *the marriage mart*."

"Perhaps you will make the acquaintance of an attractive widow while you are here in Bath, Uncle?" he suggested. "I understand that many single women prefer the quieter lifestyle to be found here. It is certainly less expensive than London."

He chuckled. "Quite an impression I make,

slouching across the chair in the Pump Room with my leg elevated on a stool. I suppose a mature, well-intentioned lady might take pity on me and strike up a conversation."

Frederick grinned. "I promise to keep watch for an unattached woman without affectations and who has a pleasing appearance as well."

"Ha! If you are lucky enough to chance upon such a one, send her my way!"

Chapter Four

The morning after arriving in Bath, Camille joined Ellen and her mother in the entryway of their temporary residence in the Royal Crescent. Their accession had gone smoothly. The butler, after offering a dignified welcome, informed them his name was Bowles. He came with the dwelling as well as two footmen, a cook, and three chamber maids.

"Camille, you and Miss Cather will wish to walk to the Pump Room. I have ordered a chair," Lady Collins advised. "I will meet you both there."

"Very well, Mother," she answered, buttoning her Corbeau colored pelisse trimmed in gold braid over her walking gown before placing her straw poke bonnet on her head and tying the matching ribbon under her chin. "Are you ready, Ellen?"

"Yes, I am." She tugged the sleeves on her violet-hued pelisse down over her wrists and looped the strings on her reticle over one arm. "I look forward to seeing the lovely limestone buildings in the morning sunshine."

"Should we visit the library and reading rooms that adjoin the Pump Room and look for a book on the architecture of Bath?" Camille suggested as Bowles opened the front door with a flourish. "I understand the proprietor, Mr. Meyler, is also a bookseller and printer."

"You have done your research well, Camille. I am quite pleased." Lady Collins gave her a warm smile, as she followed them outside. "I also recommend Mr. H. Godwin's Library on Milson Street."

"Thank you for your praise, Mother," Camille replied, with a grin. "But surely you comprehend I would never visit a city without knowing where the booksellers and libraries were located."

The sedan chair arrived for Lady Collins. Once she was stowed inside and borne away, Camile and her companion strolled past the wide expanse of green grass in front of their dwelling, then along Brock Street when they came upon the elegant homes in The Circus.

"Such lovely residences!" exclaimed Ellen. "Perhaps we will become acquainted with someone who lives here, and we may view the interiors."

"A fortunate opportunity, indeed," agreed Camille. "I understand the homes in Queen Square are also quite stately."

"Oh, yes!" enthused her companion. "I have heard only the most affluent can afford to maintain quarters there."

"Well then, I suggest we do all we can to further an introduction to people who lodge there," teased Camille, as they continued their walk down Gay Street.

Ellen giggled and reached out to put her gloved hand on Camille's forearm. "I know you too well. You are saying so only because you wish to torment me for my excessive impetuosity."

"No! Not at all!" she countered. "Rather, I envy your fervor and yearn for a smattering of vivacity myself."

"Do not talk so, dear friend!" Ellen paused, giving her an intent stare. "I know on our journey here, you claimed you were tired because of a lack of sleep. I have never seen you so out of sorts. Is there something wrong,

Camille?"

Not ready to confide her confused feelings about Frederick, she evaded answering Ellen's query. "I am experiencing a city I have never visited before. I tend to observe my surroundings and become comfortable in the setting before disclosing to others my observations and opinions. My goodness! Is that a push chair?"

They were just coming upon a street with large, elegant homes encompassing a center square plot of lush green grass and full, leafy elm trees. A tall man with broad shoulders pushed a chair with wheels down the cobbled street in front of them. The occupant of the contraption appeared to be a young lady. Her countenance, wan and placid, her frame quite slender; the gown she wore hung loosely across her small form. A thick, woolen blanket covered her legs. A maid in uniform walked at her side, frequently glancing in an apprehensive manner, at her charge.

"I am certain it will not be the last one you see," observed Ellen. "They are frequently referred to as Bath Chairs. Many people visit here for health reasons and need to use them."

"You recall, my brother required one last year after he injured his leg. I had not realized they were used as common practice."

"I understand application of the chair is becoming more redundant. When someone is considerably weakened after a prolonged illness or in the case of a broken bone which needs to be kept fixed and secure, as in your brother's situation, the advantages are obvious."

They continued to follow the group down the sloping hill until they reached Westgate Street. Lady Collins emerged from her sedan chair.

"I recollected we are required to enter our names and place of residence in the guest book if we wish to participate in the dances, balls, card assemblies or attend the concerts and lectures," Lady Collins commented with a frown, as she joined them. "It would not be proper if we neglected to do so and offended the Master of Ceremonies."

"Ellen and I will see to it after we have drunk our obligatory glass of water," Camille offered.

Lady Collins sighed. "Thank you, my dear. That would be most obliging of you. Shall we go in?"

Camille noted the semi-circular glass fanlight above the lofty, wooden double doors as they walked across the threshold. Once inside, she marveled at the high ceiling and large, paned glass windows framed by Corinthian columns. On the opposite wall, two fireplaces glowed. Nearby, a crowd of people gathered in front of a protruding room encased by an intricate bay window. At each end of the room, there were curved, distended niches. One contained a beautiful longcase clock and directly above it, perched inside an elevated bower, there was a statue of a man dressed in elegant Georgian finery. At the opposite end, on a raised balcony, encircled by intricate ironwork, a violinist and a flutist played a lovely, soothing melody.

"Lady Collins! Wonderful to see you!" gushed a slender, smiling matron with abundant golden tresses, braided, and fastened with a shell comb on the crown of her head. She strode up to their group.

"Ruth! Mrs. Warwick!" Her mother reached out to touch the woman's arm. "I apologize for coming to see you with so little notice."

"You are welcome to visit me anytime," the other

lady assured her. She turned to study Camille and Ellen. "Your daughter has inherited the famous Collins' green eyes."

Lady Collins chuckled. "Yes, she has. Camille, you were too young to remember Mrs. Warwick when she last visited us in London. And this is Miss Ellen Cather."

They both murmured acknowledgements to her.

"It has been many years," agreed Mrs. Warwick. She swiveled around, gesturing to a group of young people standing behind her. "This is my son, Herbert and my daughter, Honora. My niece, Miss Priscilla Talbot, is taking a sojourn with us for a few weeks."

As she greeted them, Camille covertly studied each one in turn. Miss Warwick had the same wavy, golden locks as her mother. Hers were gathered haphazardly together in a bun at the back of her head. Her complexion was rosy, her nose short with an unfortunate tendency to bend upward at its end. Her brown eyes sparkled impishly as a regal matron sporting a huge scarlet feather sticking out from her turban walked by. She wore a grey kerseymere pelisse trimmed in ruby-colored velvet on the bottom of the wide skirt, on the cuffs and at the shoulders.

Her brother, Mr. Warwick, was of medium height and quite stout. He had thick, dark brown hair brushed to a point in the center of his wide forehead so that it perched there, over his eyes in a tangled cluster. His ears protruded outward from behind bushy sideburns. An ostentatious cravat, tied in the mail coach style, hung at his throat. He wore a silk, sea-green coat with a wide collar with long tails and fingered an elaborate fob attached to a quizzing glass. It dangled from underneath a garish pistachio-colored waistcoat. His knee breeches struggled to contain a protruding belly. He had belted black pumps on his feet. One of his burly legs was bent forward while he affected a disinterested, bored, man-of-the-world expression.

Miss Talbot had curly, auburn brown hair gathered into a tousled mass at the crown of her head. Tiny earlobes peeked out from underneath the ringlets that framed her round face. Thick brown brows hovered over her tapered, hazel eyes. She had on a jonquil muslin walking gown ornamented at the bottom with four rows of decorative trimming. She wore an open robe over the gown, sculpted with elegant lace edges. Her arms and bust were covered with a bottle-green spencer. It had a plaited front and fastened at the center with a silver clasp in the shape of a bird.

"I'm told we met when I was three years old," Miss Warwick informed her. "I must admit I cannot recall the occasion."

Camille smiled at her while pondering if the lady was serious or poking fun. "I am not surprised. At the advanced age of four, I do not remember the event either."

"Miss Cather, are you related to a Mr. Benjamin Cather? We were school chums at Harrow," Mr. Warwick boasted while he raised his quizzing glass to one eye.

"No. I am sorry. I am not acquainted with the gentleman."

"No cause to feel sorrow, I assure you." He swung the glass around his index finger. "Lost touch with him a year or so ago. Heard he had been confined to a home. Brains were addled, don't you know."

"Oh, how terribly unfortunate." Ellen paused for a

moment and cleared her throat. "Miss Talbot, where are you from?"

"I live in Salisbury. My father is the dean there. May I ask where you live, Miss Cather?"

"My family has a small estate on the outskirts of London, in Richmond."

Miss Talbot trained her gaze upon her. "Is it true you reside for the most part in London, Miss Collins?"

"My mother and I tend to divide our time equally between the city and my brother's estate in Horsham." What started as polite conversation was rapidly becoming tedious. Camille looked over her head at the crowd of people gathered around the bay window. "Is there something of interest across the room?"

Miss Talbot tittered and then announced in a loud, boisterous voice for all around them to hear, "We have a fledgling in our midst! Obviously, this is your first visit to the Pump Room. The ladies and gentlemen are queuing to drink the renowned Bath water. You must have a glass."

Camille clamped her lips together to stifle a groan and quickly scanned the cluster of people nearby to see if anyone had taken notice of Miss Talbot's strident, churlish comment. She started with surprise as she observed the same gentleman who had been pushing the frail woman in the chair earlier, staring intently at her. She noted dark-brown eyes under thick ebony brows, curly hair of a dusky, onyx hue much like coal, worn long over his ears and collar, a commanding nose that flared at its end and full lips over a jutting chin. He wore black pantaloons and a black coat without a waistcoat. His white linen shirt did little to conceal his powerful, muscled chest. He sported a deep red cravat tied carelessly around his neck with a simple knot. He raised one sardonic brow as if to mock her interest as she completed her inspection.

Turning away from the gentleman's piercing gaze, she addressed Ellen, "I am going to procure a taste of the water. Will you join me?"

"Gladly!"

Camille led the way across the room toward the cluster of people. As they were about to pass by the unsettling gentleman, the frail lady in the push chair at his side suddenly dropped her shawl to the floor at Camille's feet. She reached down to pick up the garment.

"You dropped your shawl, ma'am."

"Oh. Thank you so much," the lady murmured, with a hesitant smile at her as she gripped it with shaking hands. "You are both wearing such lovely garments. I have been admiring them since we arrived."

"Perhaps the ladies would like to join us? It would give you an opportunity to learn the name of their seamstress," the man accompanying her suggested, as he moved the push chair backward to give them more room.

"Would you please?" the lady pleaded. "We just arrived in Bath yesterday. There has been no opportunity to meet others. I am Miss Julianna Vane. This is my brother Mr. Harcourt Vane and my nurse Miss Sims."

"I am Miss Collins, and this is Miss Cather. We came yesterday as well."

"Have you had an opportunity to purchase a subscription for the pleasure of tasting the delicious water?" Mr. Vane queried, in a cynical tone.

"No...No," Camille stammered. "I hadn't realized I needed to do so. I thought to leave a farthing or a pence."

"That won't do at all." He scowled at her and turned

to the nurse. "Miss Sims, please stay with my sister. I will escort Miss Collins to the subscription table. We will return momentarily."

Ellen held out her hand, clutching several coins. "Will you procure a card for me as well?"

"Yes, of course."

"Shall we?" Mr. Vane swung his arm outward with a flourish.

"I am sorry to be such a nuisance," she murmured to him, placing her gloved hand on his forearm. "You should not leave your sister's side."

"I assure you I am able to determine for myself the vulnerability of the present situation." He stopped his forward progress, looking down at her. "I have concluded it is perfectly acceptable to escort you to the other side of the room."

She studied his brooding countenance for a moment, experiencing a sudden flutter of surprise in her chest as she noted his heavily lined forehead and specks of gray in his curling hair. He was much older than she had first surmised. "Very well, sir."

He sighed. "I must apologize as well. My sister…she nearly died. I have been overcome with worry for many weeks. Now that she is on the mend, I find it hard to shake off the cloak of anguish that surrounded me for so long."

She gazed up into his dark brown eyes, noting their muted, murky hue. All radiance was gone. It was as if the pleasure and delight in living had escaped him. Even his full lips were lifted into the semblance of a bitter smile. She reached out with her free hand to touch his shoulder. "You must turn your thoughts away from what could have happened to your sister. Concentrate instead on experiencing the joy of knowing she will live. Cherish the additional time you now have to spend with her."

He cleared his throat. "Thank you for your kind words of advice. I promise I will do all I can to lift the dark cloud that has enveloped me. Come, here is the table."

The front door opened wide at that moment. A lady's tinkling laugh rang out over the sound of the music.

"I don't know how to thank you!" the woman exclaimed, stepping over the threshold.

"Would you consent to my escort this morning as payment for the debt?" rejoined a familiar gentleman's voice from behind the door.

"That would be lovely. I will happily accept your offer," responded the lady, with a chuckle.

Chapter Five

Knowing that his uncle wouldn't require his presence until later in the morning, Frederick made an early start the next day. Soon after finishing his breakfast, he set out to visit the Pump Room to sample the famed Bath water. He passed by several interesting shops on Milsom Street as well as a library. He made a mental note of their location, vowing to return shortly to peruse their wares.

He crossed Westgate Street, noting the impressive facade of the Bath Abbey. Suddenly, a lady's shrill yelp disturbed his pleasant ruminations.

"No! Stop! Go away!"

He darted forward, observing two mangy hounds chasing each other through the street, heedless of anyone or anything that might impede the pursuit. One circled the woman, hiding behind her skirts as the other dog stood his ground in the middle of the street, barking loudly at his tormentor. Frederick made a fist with one of his hands and raised it over his head, glaring at the agitated animal. "Here now! Be gone!"

The dog's ears stood up straight at his menacing tone and the hound loped away down the street with his furry partner following close behind.

"Gracious me!" the lady gasped, gripping her reticule with trembling fingers.

Frederick walked up to her and bowed. "Are you

hurt, ma'am?"

"No." She looked down at her gown. "Thankfully, my garment appears to have escaped damage."

He studied her. She was remarkably composed considering the recent disturbance. Of medium height, slender, with quite pale, creamy skin, her hair was brown, highlighted with flecks of red. She wore it parted in the middle, the straight locks bordered her face, the long ends clustered into a neat bundle at the crown of her head. She had an oval-shaped face, brown eyes, a long nose that flared at its tip, a small mouth, framed by modest pink lips. "Are you certain you feel no ill effects?"

"I am well," she replied in a sanguine manner.

"May I conduct you to your destination then?"

"I am at my destination." She pointed to a building close by with several Corinthian columns fronting the doorway. "The Pump Room."

"Capital! I am headed there." He smiled at her. "Take my arm."

"I don't know how to thank you!" she exclaimed, laughing as she stepped over the threshold.

"Would you consent to my escort for the morning as payment for the debt?" he offered as he followed her inside the building.

"That would be lovely. I will happily accept your offer," she replied, with a chuckle.

"Frederick....? Lord Surd?"

He flinched in surprise when he heard Camille's lovely voice. Whirling around, he observed her standing with her hand on a tall, somber gentleman's arm. The sudden sting of jealousy almost brought him to his knees. His heart squeezed inside his chest, and he struggled to breathe. "Cam…Miss Collins! I…I hoped I would chance upon you."

She frowned at him and then gazed at something beyond his right shoulder. "Indeed?"

He turned to locate the source of her exasperation and noted the woman he had rescued moments before, standing mute at his side. "Forgive me. May I present…"

"Mrs. Hervey."

"Mrs. Hervey. This is Miss Collins."

Camille nodded and pursed her lips before replying, "Lord Surd, Mrs. Hervey, may I introduce Mr. Vane. He informed me I needed to purchase a subscription first in order to sample the water."

Mrs. Hervey curtsied to them.

"How do you do?" Frederick bent at the waist.

Mr. Vane bowed. "Lord Surd, Mrs. Hervey."

Frederick studied Camille's flushed cheeks, wondering if the reason for her uneasiness meant she was discomposed by his sudden appearance, or could it be something else, given she was in the company of an attractive gentleman? "I must procure a subscription as well."

She looked away from him. "Mother is on the other side of the room. Miss Cather is over near the bow window. You will wish to greet them."

"Of course. Allow me to escort Mrs. Hervey to her friends first." He guided her forward into the center of the room.

"I don't require your assistance," Mrs. Hervey refuted. "I will settle myself."

"Nonsense." Once he stated an intention, it would be unthinkable for him not to follow through on it. "Advise me where you would like to go. Are any of your acquaintances here?"

She sighed. "As a general rule, I keep to myself."

"What of your husband?"

"I am a widow," she murmured. "My husband was killed at Waterloo."

"Oh, I am sorry." He reached out to tap her forearm. "Please forgive my gauche comment."

"Perfectly understandable. The two of you were not acquainted. Thank you for your kind sentiments." She cleared her throat. "Please take me to one of the empty chairs close to the musicians. You must carry on and offer your compliments to the others."

He guided her to a seat. "I will return after I have acknowledged them and obtained a subscription for the waters. May I bring you a glass?"

"There is no need for you to come back," she admonished. "I will be perfectly fine here on my own."

He smiled at her. She didn't know him well enough to realize it was pointless to argue. "Would you like some water?"

A burst of laughter emerged from her mouth. "Yes. Thank you."

First, he strode across the room to pay his respects to Camille's mother. Then he offered a hasty bow and greeting to Miss Cather. Before making his way back to the subscription table near the door, he intended to speak to Camille. He glanced around the room and saw her standing in one of the niches near the longcase clock. He strode over to her.

"Miss Collins."

She started at the sound of her name, whirling around to face him.

"You certainly wasted no time following me here,"

she retorted, frowning. "Or perhaps another lady holds your interest?"

"Another…?" He had no idea who she was referring to and chose to ignore the puzzling comment. "I wished to assure you I have no intention of shadowing your every move. My uncle is staying here in Bath for a time. He is suffering from a disagreeable case of gout. He requested my companionship for a few weeks. Know only that I am here in the city if you should require my assistance."

"I am sorry to hear of your uncle's suffering. I apologize for jumping to the conclusion you pursued me." She paused, her cheeks flushing pink. "I must sound like the worst kind of conceited shrew."

"Not at all," Frederick assured her, with a grin. "I have a favor to ask of you. May I occasionally join you and your acquaintances when you plan to attend evening entertainments?"

"Of course, I would enjoy having you as one of our party." She encouraged him with a smile. "Did your uncle procure rooms or a house?"

"He acquired a small townhouse on Alfred Street quite close to the Assembly Rooms."

"A very fine location. I told you previously, we were able to secure a townhouse in the Royal Crescent. I have a sense it is not too far from Alfred Street."

"I believe you are a few blocks away. Did you sample the waters?" he asked her with brows raised.

She wrinkled the tip of her adorable button nose and giggled. "Yes, I did. I will simply say, I trust the benefits are much better than the taste."

"Indeed." He grinned at her, bowed, and reached for her hand, putting her gloved fingers to his lips. "Thank you for the subtle forewarning."

"Frederick...Lord Surd?"

He raised up to gaze intently into the depths of her brilliant green eyes. "Yes, Miss Collins?"

"I wished to mention..." She paused. "While I do not anticipate requiring help, thank you for your offer. I feel comforted knowing you are close by."

He smiled as he made a deliberate, gradual movement, inconspicuously caressing her fingers before releasing her hand. "Your words bring me great assurance. It is my sincere hope my presence will always be a source of pleasure to you."

He bowed again and forced himself to walk away from her to the subscription table. He must be cognizant of the aspiration he just made and be careful not to impose or burden Camille with his attendance too frequently during her stay in Bath. After handing over a few coins to the lady at the table, he received his card and joined the short queue adjacent to the bow window enclosure. When he reached the front of the line, a woman picked up an empty glass from a nearby tray and bent over a Grecian-urn styled pump to dispense the water once his subscription card was presented to her. "May I have two glasses, please?"

He carried the small containers of water back to the seating area where Mrs. Hervey was waiting for him. He paused directly in front of her and bowed while holding out one glass. "Here you are."

"Thank you." She wrapped her gloved fingers around the vessel.

He raised his glass up in front of his face, studying the murky liquid inside. "Is there a recommended method to consuming this?"

She frowned. "I am not aware of any advised process. However, I would counsel you not to smell the water before swallowing it. The odor can be quite repugnant."

He grimaced, looking down at her in consternation. "Indeed?"

"It has been likened to rotten eggs."

She made the astonishing statement with a somber expression on her face, but he also observed the upward pull of her lips at the corners of her mouth.

"Are you provoking me, or do you speak the truth?" he inquired with one brow raised.

She smiled at him, murmuring her reply. "I assure you, my lord, I am serious."

He bent over, whispering into her ear, while holding his glass aloft. "Your comments strike me as coming from someone with little enthusiasm for the far-reaching, continually acclaimed benefits of drinking the Bath waters."

She hitched her shoulders. "Some swear by the water's healing properties. However, I have also heard of upset stomachs after drinking it. Others report no ill effects or benefits at all."

"I will drink it and hope for the best." He raised the glass to his lips and swallowed the liquid.

"What is your opinion?"

He pressed his lips together, pondering his assessment. "I am surprised by the warm temperature. I hadn't contemplated that. Certainly, there is a metallic flavor as well. It is hard to imagine this foul-tasting stuff will cure any ailment."

"The expression on your face…" She chuckled. "I believe the notion the water is an antidote for various disorders is more of a myth than an interpretation based on facts."

He frowned down at her. "Are you suggesting hordes of people make their way here each day to faithfully drink a glass of the Bath spring water, most knowing the liquid will not improve their health?"

"Surely, you cannot find the idea absurd?" She flushed, looking away from him. "Pardon me, I have no doubt you hail from London. I must appear backward, even rusticated to voice such outlandish opinions. I realize it is not the thing to openly criticize the accepted norms in society."

"Not at all. You must not berate yourself," he countered. "I have always admired those who discuss their own thoughts and beliefs on a range of subjects no matter if it is something held sacred in the social sphere. In fact, my….one of my close acquaintances rarely concerns herself with what is generally agreed upon if the practice or belief is easily refuted."

She twisted around to study him. "I am inclined to believe your friend is close to your own age. Quite a refreshing and unique trait in a young lady. As a mature woman, I must admit I am encouraged to know there are some in the adolescent set who do not follow society's creeds with a blind acceptance."

At her reference to age, he studied her complexion. He was surprised to observe traces of wrinkles at the corners of her eyes. He had assumed she was a youthful widow. "I can assure you, ma'am, the members of London society are not all empty-headed, shallow people."

"I must accept your opinion as fact because it is doubtful if I ever have a chance to visit the metropolis again. There is absolutely no need for you to continue to keep me company, my lord. The others in your party will wonder at your absence."

"To the contrary," he objected. "I promised to be your escort this morning. I never, ever renege on a pledge. Tell me, after you have taken the obligatory glass of water, how do you normally pass the remainder of the day?"

"I apprehend my appeals to you are fruitless." She sighed. "If the weather is fine, I take a stroll in Sydney Gardens. If I require some new reading material, I often browse at Mr. H. Godwin's library on Milson Street."

"Capital! I had intended to stroll down Milson Street myself to see the shops." He put his empty glass on a nearby table and then held out his arm to Mrs. Hervey. "Come along and show me the sights."

Chapter Six

Camille forced herself to contemplate the intricacies of the long case clock in front of her even as the vexatious sounds of Mrs. Hervey's chuckles and sighs reached her ears. She pondered the plausible location of the lady's husband. There was no hovering companion or nurse to be seen. Could he have sent her here alone to recover from an illness? Most improbable. Surely, her husband would stay with her until she fully regained her health? Was Frederick an acquaintance of Mr. Hervey? She couldn't recall him mentioning anyone by that name.

A flicker of movement caught at the edge of her vision. Mrs. Hervey stood up from her chair, reaching out to grasp Frederick's arm with a twinkle in her eyes and a warm smile on her lips.

Camille gasped, turning away, and closing her eyes as she struggled for breath. Her chest felt tight and compressed as if a carriage wheel had just rolled across her upper body.

"My sister is concerned that you will believe we are ignoring you. She sent me to keep you company."

She wrenched her eyelids open, discerning Mr. Vane standing at her side. She cleared her throat, forcing words from her mouth. "Pardon...I'm sorry."

His despondent expression switched to one of concern. "May I be of assistance?"

She took a deep breath, choking and then gasping

for air. "Give me a moment, please."

He stuck out his arm. "You can hold onto my sleeve if you need support."

She ignored his offer, instead gripping her hands together in front of her. "This…This clock is quite unusual. I was observing the words on the dials at the top."

He studied her and then turned toward the piece. "I understand it is a Thomas Tompion invention. He is reputed to be The Father of English Clockmaking. You refer to the words, *sun slower, sun faster?* I believe the sun is considered 'fast' during certain times of the year. During those times, the sun noon, the point at which its location is directly overhead, will reach that point a few minutes before twelve o'clock on a timepiece."

"Quite interesting. Thank you for enlightening me." She glanced at the front entrance, perceiving Frederick and his companion strolling out through the doorway. He laughed at a comment Mrs. Hervey made just before they turned and made their way down the street. Camille took another deep breath.

"Do you know the identity of this jaunty fellow?" Mr. Vane pointed to the marble figure of a Georgian gentleman tucked away in a nook above the clock.

"I understand he was known as Beau Nash," she replied, grateful for the distracting topic. "I believe he was a celebrated Master of Ceremonies here in Bath in the late 1600's."

"Correct. Richard was his first name. He was notable for encouraging an informality in manners. When visiting the city, he believed people from all levels of society should mingle and converse," he explained. "The division of the nobility and the gentry from the middle class tended to be relaxed while he was in control."

She frowned. "Admirable, but you paint a picture of a domineering gentleman."

Mr. Vane chuckled. "You have him pegged. He matched ladies with suitable dancing partners, brokered marriages, escorted unaccompanied wives, regulated gambling, and made a point to meet new arrivals in order to judge their suitability to join the select company of those who had pre-booked tables for special concerts and events."

"He sounds full of self-importance. Surely, the man had a vice?"

"He did. I understand he was a notorious gambler. He ran up so many debts, he could no longer afford to pay for his lodgings and was forced to move in with his mistress."

"The man felt justified overseeing those who bet on games of chance, but he failed to show restraint and manage his own weakness at the tables? Preposterous!"

He nodded. "I agree. However, I must give the man a hearty measure of commendation. Regardless of the gaming weakness, his enterprise to become the most celebrated arbitrator of social activities in Bath was most successful."

"Hence, the monument to him placed here in the Pump Room." She studied the marble statue, noting Richard Nash's thick, curling locks, plain coat and long waistcoat worn unbuttoned just below his protruding belly. His neck was wrapped with a modest stock, fastened with a buckle embellished around the edges with some type of jewel. His shirt was adorned with lace, falling in a majestic manner across his chest and wrists.

He clutched a tricorne hat in his left hand and his stocky legs were covered to just below the knee with tight breeches. On his feet were buckled, low-heeled shoes. "Quite the dandy."

He grinned. "I imagine he had a very high opinion of his countenance and form."

"Doubtless," she replied in a cynical tone. "I should rejoin Miss Cather and check on my mother."

"I will escort you." He offered her his arm and they strolled toward the others. "It is time for my party to return to our residence. I imagine my sister is tired from the morning's exertions."

"Oh!" She pursed her lips. "I am sorry! I never intended to keep you from her side for such an extended period."

He stopped walking, glaring down at her. "It is not my intention to place blame on you for the situation. I am told by my sister's physician that it will be some time before her spirits are fully restored. Until that happens, it is to be expected she will be weary after spending time in company without the opportunity of repose."

"I am remorseful for misunderstanding you. Perhaps it would be less distressing if you were to insist that she forego venturing outside for a time until she has fully recovered?" she suggested as they made their way past several groups of people to the other side of the room.

"It would certainly provide me much less apprehension if I were to order her to stay in her room. I must also acknowledge, however, if you were better acquainted with Julianna, you would never propose such an undertaking."

She chuckled. "Is she a stubborn lady?"

He grunted. "Obstinate, determined, relentless are

only a few of the words that come to mind."

She smiled up at him as they reached the others. "You have your hands full then."

"Indeed," he agreed with a wry twist of his lips.

"There you are!" Miss Vane clapped her hands together and bent over in her chair toward Camille. "I hope I did not overstep myself, Miss Collins, by sending my brother to keep you company?"

"Not at all. I benefited from his understanding of the city's past. He disclosed and explained some notable facts about the clock and Mr. Nash that I had no prior knowledge of."

"I am quite pleased to hear that," Miss Vane answered in a self-satisfied manner.

"You must impart what you learned to me," implored Ellen. "I wish to understand all I can about Bath while I am here."

"I would be happy to do that," Camille assured her friend. "Presently, we should join my mother and inquire as to her plans for the afternoon."

"You will both attend the dress ball on Monday evening at the Assembly Rooms? It is my birthday." Miss Vane directed a glowing smile at her brother. "Harcourt has graciously allowed me to make an appearance, if only to observe the dancing."

"Your birthday as well as a ball? How wonderful!" Ellen turned to Camille. "We must be certain to be present."

"Have you entered your names in Mr. Heaviside's book? He is the Master of Ceremonies presiding over the Upper Rooms," explained Miss Vane. "Once he knows of your arrival and place of residence, he will visit you and sanction your attendance at the balls, concerts, lectures and teas held there."

"My mother mentioned the book," Camille replied. "Do we find it in the Upper Rooms?"

"No, no. That location would not be convenient for those such as yourselves who are newly arrived in town," Miss Vane refuted, pointing one gloved finger to a spot across the room. "It is just there on the pedestal in front of the window. Be certain to write your names in Mr. Marshall's folio as well. He presides over the Lower Rooms."

"It is time for us to return home," announced Mr. Vane, as he stepped behind his sister's push chair and put his hands on the metal bar at the back.

"Must we go?" Miss Vane twisted around in her seat, frowning at her brother.

"You have not yet regained all of your former strength," he retaliated. "It would never do to overtire yourself. We will come again the day after tomorrow."

"Very well," she sighed and turned to face Camille. "Miss Collins, would you and Miss Cather come and visit me in the morning?"

Camille shared a look with Ellen. "We would be honored to call. However, your brother and nurse should first agree to the suitability of our visit."

Mr. Vane glanced at Miss Sims. "What is your opinion, Nurse? If Julianna rests quietly in her room for the remainder of the day and sleeps well tonight, may she receive visitors tomorrow?"

"Yes, of course," the lady agreed with a stern expression as she gazed at her charge. "Repose the remainder of the day and have the benefit of undisturbed slumber tonight, Miss Vane. Then you will be capable of entertaining on the morrow."

"Which means I do not want to see candlelight coming from under your door when I retire this evening," Mr. Vane admonished. "Put that Gothic romance away and go to sleep!"

"But the story is extraordinary and vastly enthralling, Brother!" she pleaded.

"Juliana, you expressed a wish to host your new friends," he reminded her, in a gruff, whispered tone. "Have you modified the notion?"

"No, no, certainly not!" She sighed, holding out both her gloved hands to Camille and Ellen. "Please come visit me. We reside in The Circus. Number thirty, just off Gay Street. I promise to do as they say!"

Camille clutched Miss Vane's fingers in her own. "We thank you for your invitation and give you our pledge to be there."

"I look forward to the opportunity to hear more of your home in Devon," Ellen assured her.

"Wonderful!" Miss Vane put her handkerchief up to her mouth, in an unsuccessful attempt to conceal a yawn. She then offered them a wavering smile. "I admit, I am fatigued. I will see you both on the morrow. Please come as early as you can."

"It was a pleasure meeting you both." Mr. Vane proffered them a brusque nod before swiveling the Bath chair around toward the entrance. The sea of people crowding the room in front of him hastened to move out of the way as he made an undeviating passage to the door.

Camille turned to Ellen. "Devon?"

"Yes, they reside there. Apparently, Mr. Vane owns and operates a cooper mine in the city of Tavistock near the canal. Until her illness, Miss Vane kept the reins of her brother's household entirely in her hands."

"Interesting. Is there no Mrs. Vane?"

"There was. She passed away five years ago of scarlet fever, the sickness that plagued Miss Vane."

"Goodness! No wonder he is so concerned over his sister's welfare after losing his wife to the same illness."

"According to Miss Vane, the death of his wife broke her brother's heart. They had only been married a short time when she became ill."

"I am extremely sorry for him." Camille sighed. "The gentleman certainly has had more than his share of grief and worry."

"Have I upset you?" Ellen asked with concern. "Do you wish to forego visiting the reading rooms?"

"No, not at all! I would welcome the distraction. I wish to procure a book on the history of Bath. I need to brush up on my knowledge of the city if I hope to maintain a semblance of intelligence when conferring with Mr. Vane."

Her companion raised her brows. "Is it important to you to impress him with your perception and wit?"

"Certainly. It would never do to have Mr. Vane believe I have no interests in life other than the fabric on my gown or the arrangement of my hair," she retorted. "We must enter our names in the guest books before locating Mother and informing her of our plans."

Chapter Seven

Frederick kept his gaze trained on the busy scene outside the Pump Room. Several elderly ladies were being helped from their chairs by the attendants. It would be inadvisable to glance back at Camille. Even though she agreed to his presence for occasional evening entertainments, he sensed he was not welcome to continually hover at her side or give excessive notice while in her vicinity. He turned to his companion, recalling his intention to squire her down Milsom Street.

"Where should we begin?" he inquired. "Is there a particular shop you wish to visit?"

Mrs. Hervey pursed her trim lips before speaking. "If it would not be an inconvenience, I need to collect a pair of slippers I had repaired at Joseph Cooper's shop on Bridge Street."

"Of course. Show me the way."

She placed her hand on his outstretched arm. "I would also like to purchase a pair of gloves at the hatter and glove seller next door to Mr. Cooper's shop."

"I sense Milsom Street is not the only place in the city to find an assortment of things to purchase?"

"It is certainly not the sole location to find items of interest," she affirmed. "A favorite shop of mine to browse in is called S. & J. Martin. They are located at 23 Milsom Street and specialize in fine jewelry as well as small trinkets, silver pieces such as toast racks, tea and coffee urns, butter coolers. Of interest are their toothpick cases and snuff boxes. They are also watchmakers."

"That sounds quite interesting. Let us make a point of stopping there. I am impressed by the assortment of goods offered in this city. I imagine there is a modicum of entertainment to choose from in the evenings?"

"Not at all. There are concerts, balls, the theatre, and numerous lectures to attend. This is Mr. Cooper's shop." She indicated a weathered door with a carved piece of wood in the shape of a boot hanging on it. A few pairs of shiny men's boots, some ladies' slippers as well various shapes and sizes of women's pattens were on display in the shop's window. "Are you going to wait outside?"

"No, no." He reached past her to push open the door. "I intend to join you. I would take great pleasure in the opportunity to examine Mr. Cooper's selection of boots more closely."

She tilted her head to one side, pondering him without speaking.

"Is there something wrong?"

"No, no. I suddenly had a fanciful notion that I had met you somewhere before." With that cryptic comment, she turned away from him and marched inside the shop.

"Welcome, Mrs. Hervey," boomed a portly jovial man from behind the counter. "Your slippers are finished. Good as new, they are!"

"Thank you, Mr. Cooper. It will be lovely to wear them again. They are my favorite, most comfortable pair."

Frederick strolled inside behind her and picked up a boot that was one of a pair he saw in the window. He studied the craftmanship.

"You interested in some boots, sir?" the shopkeeper

inquired. "Those are of quite fine quality."

"I certainly attest to that," Frederick acknowledged as he ran his fingers across the soft, pliable leather. "I wish to inquire about purchasing a pair. But please, take care of Mrs. Hervey first."

"Let me call my son to assist you. He is the sole crafter of all the footwear now. I stick to helping customers and collecting payments," the man informed him, before turning to face a curtained doorway. "Henry, look alive! This here gentleman is interested in a pair of boots."

A young man emerged from behind the curtain. In great contrast to his father, he was tall and slender. His thick hair was combed off his forehead, the loose ends rammed behind his ears. He wore an apron made of coarse material over a pair of rough breeches and a shirt that was covered in brown smudges at his wrists. "Yes, sir?"

Mrs. Hervey quickly completed her business. She clutched the wrapped parcel to her chest as she edged toward the shop door. "Lord Surd, please take your time. I will be next door."

"I…I am sorry, my lord!" The man stammered the apology when he heard his title.

Mr. Cooper puffed out his thickset chest as he stood behind the counter, rubbing his hands together. "I promise you'll never find any boots of better merit then those we sell, my lord! Even those hoity toity shopkeepers in London would find it hard to argue over our distinction!"

Frederick rotated the boot, perusing the quality of the leather as well as the heel height. "I don't imagine I will be doing much riding while I am here. I had thought to purchase a pair that are comfortable, but sturdy enough for walking on Bath's steep, uneven streets as well as being smart enough for informal evening attire."

"You can't do better than to buy ours. Notice the malleable, soft calf-skin leather, my lord? The cut is just below the knee as well, bringing more freedom of movement," Mr. Henry Cooper explained. "The heel height can be reduced if that is your preference."

"If I purchase a pair today, how long will it take to make them?"

The shoemaker glanced at his father before answering. "I could have them ready early next week, my lord."

"Excellent."

Mr. Cooper bustled out from behind the counter, dragging a dilapidated wooden chair. "Take a seat, my lord! Henry will have you measured and sized in a trice."

The proportions were quickly determined, and a price agreed upon. Frederick pulled on his boots and stood up from the chair.

"A pleasure doing business with you, my lord!" Mr. Cooper gushed and then bowed to him. "Henry will have the boots ready on Monday afternoon."

"I appreciate it. Thank you." He adjusted his coat and strode to the door, hoping he hadn't kept Mrs. Hervey waiting too long.

She emerged from the shop next door at that moment, carrying two packages in her arms. "Oh! I took some time choosing what I wanted. I was concerned you would be losing patience with me."

"As a matter of fact, I ordered a pair of boots and only now concluded the transaction." He smiled at her as he reached for her parcels. "Have you no maid? Allow me to carry those."

Her cheeks flushed as she handed him the packages. "No, I don't. I live quite simply. I have a housekeeper who answers my door, cleans the house, and assists me with my wardrobe and hair. A cook is also in residence. Her husband handles heavy lifting and repairs."

"I see." He imagined her husband had failed to provide enough funds for her to manage a well-staffed household. He held out his free arm. "Shall we?"

She gripped his sleeve but didn't move. "Before you deduce I am a poor widow on the edge of starvation, allow me to contradict that notion. Thomas put aside plenty of money to sufficiently see myself and my staff taken care of for many years to come."

"I am relieved to know your husband had such great foresight in the matter of your future needs if he should die in battle."

She gazed at him for a moment, clamping her lips together in a thin line. "I apologize for my mutinous attitude. I suffer great provocation whenever I believe anyone is grieved or remorseful over my situation. I assure you I am quite content and happy."

"No need to ask my pardon, Mrs. Hervey," he attested, making a note of her obvious sensitivity to the subject. "I am glad to hear you are well-settled. Shall we make our way to Milsom Street, or do you wish to drop off your parcels first?"

"Perhaps it is best to take them home. S. & J. Martin's shop is quite jumbled. I fear carrying the packages inside would be awkward for you as well as inconvenient. My home is just off Milsom Street. If we cross Westgate and follow Bridewell Lane to Queen Street, it is of no great distance from there."

He chuckled as they began to walk. "It is obvious you have made your home here for several years. I am familiar with the names Queen Square, The Circus and Royal Crescent, but I would be at a loss to give someone directions to any of those places. Was Bath your principal home when your husband was alive?"

"No. My husband is the youngest of three sons of the Earl of Brantford. We met at a ball in London in 1795," she explained. "Thomas was on leave from taking part fighting the French in the revolution at the time. He injured his hand falling off his horse when the animal was hit with a stray bullet and killed. We married a year later and shortly afterward he rejoined the 1st Life Guards. I stayed in London, living with various relatives while he was away. At the end of the war in 1802, we subsequently relocated to one of his father's smaller estates in Oxfordshire. He purchased the townhouse here for me in 1814 after deciding to join his regiment to assist in the fight against Napoleon. I moved to Bath almost a year after Thomas's death at Waterloo."

"It was providential he thought to acquire property and assign the title in your name. You can now live your own life without being dependent on his family," he observed.

"I will be forever grateful to him for doing so," she agreed with a sigh. "Although at the time, his decision was a hard thing to bear."

Her words surprised him. He turned to study her expression. "Indeed. Why is that?"

She averted her face, looking at the ground. "When I learned of his intention to join in the fight against Napoleon, I believed it was a validation of my worst suspicions. Thomas also left me soon after our marriage to go to battle. It was not hard to imagine I failed monstrously as a wife. He preferred fighting wars to spending time in my company."

He came to a sudden halt, causing her to look up at him in surprise. "Never say such a thing! I haven't known you long, but I am certain you could not have been the reason he returned to his regiment. Your description of his actions provides an image of a man who felt deep responsibility to fight for our country."

"When he was at home, Thomas certainly examined the newspapers for hours daily to learn the most recent information on scrimmages or battles," she admitted with a frown. "I assumed he was bored with me and the predicable daily life on the estate. It never occurred to me that he might miss being on the battlefield. Perhaps you are right. He had few responsibilities at home. His father and elder brothers shouldered most of the burdens and duties."

"We sometimes forget to put ourselves in other people's shoes and look at life from their perspectives. I have found doing so brings me clarity when I find myself questioning my friend's motives."

"A wise thing to do," she replied with a wan smile. "If I had done so with my husband, I could have saved myself much grief and anguish. Oh, we have arrived!"

Frederick studied the structure. The surface was covered in the renowned golden Bath stone. The front door was painted black and there was a curved arch accentuated with clear glass over it. Two twelve-paned windows abutted the door. One larger and wider, fifteen-paned aperture decorated the front of the middle story. It had a raised pedimented shelf held up by scrolled details underneath it. The top floor had a smaller, six-piece glass sash window. He spied the street name on a wall nearby. "This is called Quiet Street?"

She chuckled as she stepped up to the front door. "Yes. It is quiet and tiny as well. There are only ten structures on the entire street."

"It seems to be a convenient location," he observed as the door opened at her knock.

A woman well past the first blush of youth stood on the landing dressed in a black serviceable gown with a large, white apron wrapped around her ample waist, covering the skirt. "Welcome back, Mrs. Hervey."

"Beatrice, this is Lord Surd. He was kind enough to carry my parcels for me." She turned to glance at him. "This is Miss Dell, my housekeeper as well as my maid."

"I will take them, my lord." The housekeeper bobbed a curtsey and then reached out for the packages, gazing intently at him. "Would you like me to serve tea, ma'am?"

"No, no! Lord Surd and I intend to visit a few shops on Milsom Street. I will return for refreshment in an hour."

"Very well." Miss Dell gave him one last look of appraisal before turning away to disappear down a long corridor.

Frederick had a glimpse of an overstuffed sofa and matching chair, a bookcase overflowing with many books and a fireplace with a clock on the mantle decorated with a golden bird perched on top before Mrs. Hervey shut the door. "Your home appears to be cozy and comfortable."

"Oh, yes. It is quite delightful to live here." She giggled. "And so beneficial for my well-being to live on Quiet Street."

He laughed as he stepped onto the sidewalk and offered her his arm once more. "Quite advantageous indeed!"

Chapter Eight

"Isn't that Lord Surd and Mrs. Hervey coming out of that residence?" asked Ellen.

Camille looked away from studying bonnets in the shop window to see Frederick and Mrs. Hervey laughing together as they stepped away from the doorway of a nearby townhouse.

"Miss Collins, Miss Cather! Those hats are truly lovely," called out Mrs. Hervey. "Mrs. Veazy has some fine items in her shop. She also carries fashionable pieces from Paris."

"Good day," replied Ellen. "We were admiring the silk trims on the hats. The material appears quite exceptional."

"Did you see something in the window that impressed you, Miss Collins?" inquired Lord Surd with a smile.

She frowned at him, not answering his query, before scrutinizing Mrs. Hervey. "When may we have the pleasure of meeting your husband?"

The lady's creamy, opaque skin blanched. "I…I am a widow. My husband was killed in battle at Waterloo."

"Oh, I am sorry." Camille bit her lip, tasting blood. What made her so abrupt and outspoken? She must learn to deliberate over her statements and queries before she articulated them.

"I wonder if you both would like to accompany us

to a shop just down the street." Mrs. Hervey clutched her reticule with shaking fingers. "I recommended it to Lord Surd. They have quite a vast variety of items. I find it a pleasure to look at their pieces of fine jewelry as well as the smaller trinkets and baubles on display that are more affordable. There is also a large selection of tea and coffee urns."

"Oh yes! I would enjoy perusing their wares," remarked Ellen with a smile at her. "I had thought to purchase something from Bath to give to my mother."

"It is just down the street," Mrs. Hervey informed them.

"You two go on ahead," Lord Surd advised. He held his arm out to Camille. "We will follow you."

She gripped his forearm, not speaking until the others had moved away. "I apologize for causing your…your friend distress. I can say nothing in my defense other than I often speak without first ruminating about the possible consequences."

"I trust you will not cast yourself into the dismals over it," he entreated. "I made the same mistake not two hours ago."

"You surprise me!" She stared into his warm brown eyes. A gentle breeze wafted through the street provoking the yellow-gold strands of his hair to lift off his forehead.

"Mrs. Hervey and I met by chance, providing ample justification for my initial assumption she had a husband." He murmured the words, gazing intently at her. "I admire your forthright, undisguised manner. Too many young women in society prefer to put on airs while at the same time muffling themselves when a statement of opinion or belief on a particular subject is solicited from them."

She wrinkled her nose as she pictured several ladies of her acquaintance with the type of aspect he described. "I find them intolerable."

He tapped the end of her nose with one gloved finger. "You look adorable when you adopt that expression."

"Interesting." She took a step back, causing him to drop his hand from her face. "How would you describe my fetching countenance in that moment, my lord?"

He grinned at her. "A combination of annoyance, pique, and outrage."

She giggled. "Careful! Such intense flattery might make me swoon and fall to the ground at your feet."

"A development such as that would be of no inconvenience to me, Miss Collins," he retaliated, with a smile. "Rather an opportunity to pick you up and gather you close in my arms."

"Camille! Lord Surd! Are you coming?" called Ellen as she stood in front of an open shop door a short distance away.

"Oh! Yes. We will be there momentarily." She cleared her throat.

"I apologize, Miss Collins," Lord Surd asserted in a soothing, conciliating tone. "I forgot myself. I will ask Mrs. Hervey to accompany me to another shop."

All conjectures of what she had intended to say to him fled her mind. "I don't understand. Are you implying I should not associate with her?"

"Should not…?" He frowned "Not at all! Rather, I gave you the assurance earlier that I would not dog your footsteps during your visit in Bath. Yet here I am monopolizing your company."

She gave him a slow smile, reaching for his arm. "Nonsense. I enjoyed our repartee. I always delight in bantering words with you. Please do not chastise yourself."

He sighed deeply while looking down at her, his brown eyes glowing with an amber hue and placed his hand over hers. "Forgive me. My emotions careened from intense despair one moment to light-headed giddiness the next."

She laughed. "Shall I see if the others have a vinaigrette, my lord? It would not be at all the thing to continue our shopping expedition if you feel faint."

He lowered his brows and glared at her before tempering the action with a chuckle. "Are you insinuating I suffer from a delicate constitution?"

She tilted her head to one side, pretending to consider his query. "I admit a debilitating hindrance such as that would never have occurred to me. However…"

"Cease your provocation, Camille!" He leaned over, whispering the words into her ear. "I will be obligated to quiet you."

"Indeed, my lord?" she murmured, relishing enticing scents of soap and sandalwood as he bent toward her. "I cannot imagine how you would accomplish that."

"I will demonstrate one day when we are alone and behind closed doors," he taunted, before standing up straight and clearing his throat. "Come. We should scrutinize the goods in the shop."

Camille grasped the sleeve of his coat with a quivering hand, allowing Frederick to guide her down the street. His nearness and suggestive words made her feel off-center. Her face felt hot and flushed, her heartbeat reverberated loudly in her ears. It was a struggle to breathe. Unable to fasten her attention on anything other than the unfamiliar sensations coursing throughout her body, she aimlessly put one foot in front of the other in a haphazard motion, unconcerned about their intended destination.

"Here we are."

The deep, soothing resonance of Frederick's voice calmed her disordered perceptions, gradually making her aware of her surroundings. She managed to take a deep breath before walking past him as he held the shop door open for her.

"Camille! You must come! Look at the dear little earrings!"

She sauntered toward her friend and Mrs. Hervey while chastising herself for her befuddled, distracted state. Why was she reacting to Frederick in this irregular manner? She was not ready to marry and have children, yet her insides felt reduced to nothing more than a glob of jellied eel at his evocative comment. She mentally shook herself as she reached the others, attempting to concentrate on the trinkets displayed in front of her. "How lovely!"

"I especially adore these pearl-set flowers." Ellen held the earrings up for her to admire.

"The white daisy is an appropriate symbol in jewelry for a young, unmarried woman such as yourself, Miss Cather," remarked Mrs. Hervey. "It represents purity and innocence."

"I understand the daisy can also be a token of loyal love," Lord Surd commented, as he stood considering other items in a case nearby. He pointed at something with one gloved finger and turned to gaze at Camille.

"What is your opinion of this brooch, Miss Collins? It is in the shape of a forget-me-not flower set with turquoise stones."

She stepped closer, studying the piece he indicated. "It is beautiful."

"Are you aware of the representation of this flower?" he whispered the query in her ear.

She reached out to grip the edge of the counter. "Other than the obvious connotation? No."

"It is said to be a symbol of lasting, true love."

"Oh!" A sudden commotion at the front door caused her to start and move away from him. She turned around to discover the cause of the precipitous uproar.

Miss Warwick and Miss Talbot charged into the shop together, laughing in an uncontrolled, hysterical manner. Mr. Warwick lunged over the threshold just behind them. The complaisant, nonchalant aspect he assumed earlier in the Pump Room had disappeared. His face was currently an alarming shade of puce. He pulled a handkerchief from his waistcoat pocket and proceeded to wipe his forehead with shaking hands.

Miss Warwick turned to survey the room and gasped. "Miss Collins! Miss Cather! You must forgive our unseemly comportment. My brother was busy admiring the shine on his boots and he nearly fell into a puddle of mud!"

"Exceedingly droll!" chuckled Miss Talbot, gazing with interest at Lord Surd while batting her eyelashes.

"Enough of your ceaseless prattle, Honora!" declared Mr. Warwick. He put his handkerchief back in his pocket and tugged on his cravat. "Why must you make such a spectacle of all of us with your unseemly behavior? I will remind you I successfully avoided falling and coming to grief."

"So fortunate you were spared further embarrassment, Brother," agreed Miss Warwick as she nudged Miss Talbot's arm with her elbow while also staring at Lord Surd.

As the chaotic scene lapsed and the shop environment once more became calm and serene, Camille stepped forward and cleared her throat. "I believe you have not been introduced. This is Lord Surd, and this is Mrs. Hervey. May I present the son and daughter of my mother's close friend, Mr. and Miss Warwick, and their cousin Miss Talbot?"

"Charmed, Lord Surd," Miss Talbot simpered as she and Miss Warwick curtsied to him, pointedly ignoring Mrs. Hervey.

"Mrs. Hervey, a pleasure. My lord!" Mr. Warwick minced forward and flaunted a deep bow. Then he stood up straight and tall, puffing out his rotund chest. "I believe I will purchase a snuff box. Will you kindly offer me advice? What would a London swell such as yourself carry?"

"Since I do not take snuff, I would not be qualified to give my opinion." Lord Surd bowed and turned away, walking to the far end of the shop.

Camille studied Miss Warwick and Miss Talbot as they hurried over to the case displaying the jewelry. She experienced a sense of great embarrassment over their crass behavior to Mrs. Hervey. The women appeared heedless of the insult. Miss Warwick fussed over the earrings on display while Miss Talbot demanded to be shown necklaces. Not feeling equal to contending with the ladies' boisterous, callous mannerisms, Camille moved to the breadbasket and toast rack table. She picked up an elegant epergne dish stand perched at the back of the arrangement.

"Miss Collins. I wonder if you would advise me. Could you suggest a unique birthday gift for my sister?"

"Oh!" She started at the sound of Mr. Vane's voice and looked up to see him staring at her with concern. "I didn't see you come in the shop."

"I apologize. I only just arrived and thought to purchase something for Julianna now while she is resting."

"You said you are looking for something unique?"

"Yes. I usually buy her a shawl or a necklace, but this year I thought to purchase something she could use daily."

"I understand she enjoys reading. Does she draw or sketch?"

"Yes, she often spends her mornings sketching birds from her bedchamber window."

"I spotted some lovely, tooled leather portfolios." She indicated he should follow her and crossed to the other side of the shop. "Aren't these beautiful?"

He picked up a royal blue folder embossed with gold on the edges of the tooled leather binding and carefully opened the top flap. Inside was a stack of high-quality vellum and several pencils securely tucked into an adjacent pouch. "This is perfect. Thank you so much for your suggestion."

"A pleasure."

Mr. Vane called over a clerk, indicating he intended to purchase the portfolio. The man wrapped it up and told him he would return momentarily with the bill. After the purchase had been completed, Mr. Vane turned to Camille.

"Would you save me a dance on Monday evening?"

She dropped the beaded reticule she had been examining and faced him. "Why…yes, of course."

He frowned. "Do I detect hesitation in your answer? It was not my intention to force you to do anything you might consider repugnant."

"I assure you, Mr. Vane, my uncertainty was not caused by displeasure. Rather, I was surprised you intended to join in the dancing. I believed you would keep your sister company at the ball and stay at her side the entire time."

"I must apologize once again, Miss Collins. This time for my boorish mannerisms." He furrowed his dark brows together and sighed. "There is rarely opportunity at home to attend social gatherings. Overseeing the many aspects of the mine operation and its management consumes all my days. I have been widowed for more than five years as well. I am sadly out of practice with the art of coquetry."

She smiled. "I sympathize with the circumstances, sir. I promise to hold a place for you on my dance card."

A tall clock at the front of the shop sounded the half-hour.

"Is it as late as that?" Lord Surd exclaimed as he moved away from a display of toothpick holders and strode toward Mrs. Hervey. "I am sorry. I must go."

"I intended to leave as well."

"May I escort you to your home?"

"Yes. Thank you."

Camille swallowed hard and her heart clenched inside her chest as she watched Mrs. Hervey put her hand on Frederick's arm. He led her out of the shop without so much as a backward glance at her.

Chapter Nine

He found his uncle in the breakfast room, sitting with his leg propped up on a low stool, in front of a plate containing eggs and toast. Frederick strode inside. "I sincerely apologize for the lateness of the hour, Uncle."

He dropped his fork, making a waving gesture with his hand. "Do not fret, Nephew. As I informed you yesterday, I never leave my room before eleven. I understand you broke your fast earlier. Have a cup of coffee or some ale. Tell me, do you find Bath to your liking?"

Frederick poured himself a glass of ale and took the chair across from him. "I admit I am surprised by the wealth of entertainments and enjoyable pastimes that I understand are offered in the city. The abundance of shopkeepers offering an assortment of most items one could need or wish for is also unexpected. I have ordered a pair of fine boots from a Mr. Cooper and son."

"I have heard of his exceptional footwear. Although its popularity is waning, Bath attained the impressive role of being one of Britain's largest cities a few years ago," his uncle reminded him. "It is to be expected a substantial population of people would require an array of choices for diversion as well as garments and other necessities. Did you visit the Pump Room?"

"Yes, I did." Frederick took a drink from his glass. "The famed waters do not deserve such exuberant notoriety."

"Ha! You weren't impressed? No immediate sense of health and vigor?"

"Hardly. Rather, a threatening gagging sensation from the putrid odor. I managed to stifle the temptation because there was a lady present."

"A lady? Not even a day in the city and you have made a conquest!"

"Not at all! A couple of mangy dogs were using her as a decoy in their game of chase. I happened to be nearby and came to her rescue by shooing the mongrels away. I escorted the lady to her destination, which fortuitously also happened to be the Pump Room."

"I imagine after you introduced yourselves, she presented you to her acquaintances?" His uncle took a sip of coffee.

"As a matter of fact, I came upon some friends of mine from London before I had the opportunity. She gave her name to them before the situation became awkward. A Mrs. Hervey."

"Married? An older woman?"

"She is widowed. Her husband was killed in Waterloo. I didn't notice initially, but yes, she is close to middle age."

"The lady has maintained her youthful appearance then?"

Frederick stared at his half-empty glass as he attempted to recall her features. "Her skin color is quite translucent and rather pale but except for a few fine lines on her forehead and a trace of wrinkles at the corner of her eyes, her complexion has retained a smooth, satiny appearance. Her hair is reddish brown, worn parted in the middle, gathered in a substantial bun on the crown of her head. She is of medium height, with brown eyes. Have I provided you with enough of a description, Uncle?"

He chuckled. "Yes, indeed. It seems you have a talent for keen observation. Who are the others you are acquainted with from London?"

"Lady Collins, her daughter, Miss Collins, and her friend Miss Cather. I have known the Collins family for many years. I met Miss Cather at Sir Edward Collins' summer house party last year at Horsham House."

"Wonderful!" His uncle rubbed his hands together. "I feared there would be a scarcity of eligible women in town available for dancing and other youthful pursuits to keep you expiring from boredom during your visit here. It sounds as if my concerns were for naught. You must enter your name and address in the books for both the Upper and Lower Rooms so you may be approved to participate in the social events. The Master of Ceremonies for each location will visit here and collect your subscription fee."

"Where might I find these tomes, Uncle?"

"They are kept in a place of importance in the Pump Room. We will stop by there presently. You will remember my previous remark on the benefits of bathing. If you would be good enough to accompany me, my physician recommended I take a dip twice weekly in the waters at King's Bath. The sulfuric content is said to stimulate and equalize the circulation, which is of great benefit for those of us suffering from gout. I believe you will find an advantage to the waters as well. It is also said they promote a healthy skin tone."

"I will gladly squire you there. Advise me, what is the customary bathing attire?"

"Many gentlemen wear canvas drawers, matching

waistcoats, and a fine linen cap to keep their hair dry, others sport only drawers, some are naked. There is no need to concern yourself with notions of discreetness. The men's and ladies' changing rooms and bathing pools are on opposite sides of the building. Not surprisingly, the women's section is known as the Queen's Bath. The two pools are separated by a thick marble wall."

"I look forward to the experience and believe my valet can come up with something suitable for me to wear."

A little over an hour later, Frederick emerged from the townhouse carrying a valise that contained his bathing attire. He nodded to the chairmen and then inspected the sedan chair that had been procured for his uncle's transport to the spa. Gimble and Rigsby appeared in the doorway, supporting his uncle between them. They helped him settle inside the contraption and propped his leg up on the opposite seat. Mr. Melter waved them away, admonishing the chairmen to proceed without haste. "I implore you in this because any jostling or bouncing will cause me great pain."

As Frederick strolled alongside, he noticed the chairmen took his uncle's warning to heart, navigating the narrow, steep streets with great consideration. Unfortunately, regardless of their caution, one cannot always avoid encountering inconsiderate, heedless individuals. They approached the corner of Milsom and Green Street when an imprudent young whipster, haphazardly seated upon a fractious mare, suddenly appeared. The horse charged headlong toward them.

Frederick leaped in front of the Sedan chair as the chairmen abruptly halted their forward progress. "Have a care, you inconsiderate greenhorn!"

The boy managed to yank on the reins, hauling the skittish horse away from them at the last moment, avoiding what would have certainly been a disastrous collision. "Sorry!"

Frederick didn't answer, choosing instead to glare at the youth until he was lost to sight. He turned back to the chair. "Are you hurt, Uncle?"

He bent forward, peering around the curtained window. "No, no. Just a slight twinge."

After giving the chairmen the order to proceed once more, Frederick walked in front of the chair, scanning the landscape ahead for any possible hazards. The remaining streets were traversed without further incident. The chairmen came to a stop in front of two closed doors in an alleyway just below the Pump Room.

"Take my cane, Frederick, and assist me out of this apparatus."

He offered his uncle his arm, helping him to climb out of the chair and then stand with most of the weight on his good leg. Frederick handed him his cane and tipped the chairmen. "Should I knock on the door? Which one is it?"

"Yes. The door on the left. Note the tiny letter G over the door referring to Gentlemen. One of the attending guides will let us in. There are stone steps leading down to the dressing rooms. You go ahead of me."

"Lord Surd?"

Frederick looked up and recognized the man Camille had introduced earlier. "Yes. Mr....?"

He bowed. "Vane. Are you intending to try the spa?"

"Yes. I am accompanying my uncle, Mr. Melter."

"Pleased to meet you, sir. I thought to try out the

waters while my sister is resting."

The spa door his uncle had previously indicated suddenly opened. A burly, middle-aged man stood on the threshold. "Mr. Melter, welcome."

His uncle limped forward. "Good day, Keel. Mr. Keel, this is my nephew, Lord Surd, come to try the spa with me. This other fellow goes by the name of Vane."

The man bowed. "Welcome, my lord, Mr. Vane. Please follow the steps down to the dressing rooms. They will be on your left. I will assist Mr. Melter."

"After you have changed, Frederick, you will see the entrance to the spa just beyond the fireplace," his uncle explained. "Go on in, I will join you there shortly."

Frederick made his way down the stone steps with Mr. Vane following close behind. A stooped, elderly man met them at the bottom.

"Welcome, gentlemen." He thrust out a wrinkled, heavily veined arm and pointed across the room to what appeared to be curtained alcoves. "You may disrobe in one of these rooms. When you are ready, join me here. I will be your guide in the spa."

Frederick stepped forward and pulled back the drape on one of the openings to discover a cramped space consisting of a rudimentary wooden bench over an uneven rock floor. He dropped the curtain behind him, tossed his bag onto the bench, quickly taking off his boots and stockings before stripping off his coat, shirt, and trousers. He folded all the garments into a neat pile before reaching inside the valise for the linen drawers and waistcoat his valet had procured for his use while in the water. Shivering as the damp, sulfur-infused air wafted in front of his nose, he yanked off his drawers and swiftly replaced them with the linen ones. He made short work of buttoning up the waistcoat before thrusting his clothing into the valise and grabbing his boots.

He nudged the curtain aside and found the guide waiting for him with Mr. Vane at his side, wearing only a towel wrapped across his middle. "Where do I put my garments?"

"Over here." The man shuffled across the stone floor and to a large cupboard tucked away behind a sizable boulder. The hinges creaked as he unfastened the latch and swung the door outward.

Frederick eyed several crooked, wobbly boards inside the cabinet before placing his bag on what appeared to be a fixed, solid shelf.

The man then swung the cupboard closed and latched it. He handed Frederick a towel from a neatly folded stack nearby. "Follow me, gentlemen."

They trailed behind him, walking past the roaring fireplace. Just on the other side, the rumble of male voices could easily be discerned. A few more steps down a short passage and they were inside the bathing room.

As he peered through the heavy mist, Frederick could discern approximately fifteen men in the water. Several of the bathers were accompanied by attendants. They talked in low voices to their companions while holding onto their arms, carefully guiding them around the bath.

"You gentlemen may enter whenever you are ready," advised their guide. "Make certain you do not bump into the invalids. I will alert you when twenty minutes has passed. It is not recommended to be in the spa any longer than that."

Mr. Vane untied the towel from his waist, tossing it onto a nearby bench. He quickly walked down the steps leading to the bath, submerging himself in the water.

Frederick decided to wait until his uncle joined him. He strolled over to Mr. Vane. "How is it?"

"Quite invigorating. My skin is tingling, and the warmth is soothing as well." He wrinkled his nose. "I wouldn't advise taking deep breaths. The odor is overpowering."

"Frederick, it is not necessary to wait for me."

He turned around to find his uncle standing at his side dressed in similar linen drawers and a waistcoat. He grasped his cane in one hand, holding one leg awkwardly and bent at the knee. "I wished to offer you my assistance, Uncle."

"Thank you but there is no need. Keel will help me into the spa."

"Very well." He dropped his towel and walked over to the stone steps. The first touch of the heated water on his toes was warm and comforting. As he made his way forward, around two patients and their guides, the water lapped at his thighs and then, with a few more paces, his chest. It had a heavy, dense characteristic, quite different from bath water.

"What is your assessment?"

Frederick turned to find Mr. Vane lounging on a stone ledge nearby. "I agree with you. The water is extremely soothing. I admit a sense of calmness has invaded my consciousness."

Mr. Vane chuckled. "When I tell my sister about my experience, she will insist I come here every day. She is constantly berating me for working too hard and causing myself needless disquiet and tension."

"I don't believe I met your sister."

"No." He frowned. "Juliana was at the Pump Room

this morning, but she is confined to a chair. My sister is still quite weak."

"I am sorry. She has been ill?"

"Yes. She nearly died from scarlet fever. My wife was taken by the same illness five years ago."

"A horrendous loss for you. You must have been frantic with worry for your sister."

"It was quite hard. In both cases, I wasn't allowed to visit because of concerns over transmission of the disease. I hired the best physicians I could find and immersed all my energy into work to avoid driving myself mad with worry."

"What is your occupation?"

"I own and manage a cooper ore mine in Tavistock, Devon."

"A difficult job, indeed." Frederick made his way across the spa to perch on a jutting shelf facing the entrance.

"I handle a myriad of issues," Mr. Vane conceded. "However, transporting the ore to the sea has become much easier with the building of the canal."

"Which canal, Mr. Vane?"

Frederick turned to discover his uncle, with Keel at his side, a short distance away. Keel stood next to him, holding up the ends of what appeared to be a type of sling, supporting his uncle's affected limb, just underneath the water.

"The Tavistock Canal. It opened in 1817," Mr. Vane explained. "Before it was built, the copper ore had to be transported by horse and wagon to the Morwellham Quay where it was loaded onto ships. Now, we can fill the boats at the shores of the canal near the mine entrance. They are placed in a type of rotating cradle in the water. When this occurs, the weight of the loaded boats raises the empty ones. We secure them for replenishing. The vessels packed of cooper ore follow the incline down the canal to the quay, and the crates are loaded onto the waiting ships."

"Ingenious." His uncle motioned to Keel as he slowly made his way over to the other end of the stone ledge, lowering himself onto it with a sigh. "I heard you speak of your wife's passing five years ago, a terrible tragedy. I imagine you felt her loss profoundly. A loving wife would provide much needed sympathy and understanding when you return home at night after an exhaustive day at the mine."

"You surprise me, Mr. Melter. Your thorough comprehension of my emotions is remarkable. Your wife is a lucky woman."

"I am sorry, but you offer me unjustified praise, Mr. Vane. I have never been married."

"Astonishing! Then tell me, to what do you owe your excessive sentimentality?"

"I suppose I must have an inordinately romantic nature."

"I recommend you make a point to discover a woman who speaks to your tender sensibilities and warms your heart. Marry her straightaway. Now that my sister is on the mend, I intend to remedy my bachelor status as soon as possible. As a mine owner, not only is it wonderfully sustaining to have a compassionate woman to greet me at my door when I return home after a strenuous day at work, there is also a practical issue. I am required to host dinners several times a year for investors and other business associates. I have taken advantage of my sister's agreement to act as my alternative hostess for too long."

"Miss! You have taken the wrong passage! You must not go in there!"

Frederick stood up, looking toward the sound of the man's frantic, harassed voice. Out of the corner of one eye, he spied the fleeting image of a lady covered in a gauzy morning gown with her hair tucked inside a lacy mop cap as she stepped around the fireplace. The woman's gaze appeared to gravitate to him. A sudden gust of cool air wafted across the room as if an outside door had been left open. The haze-like steam suddenly receded, and he had a clear view of the lady's features. Camille!

Chapter Ten

Camille poked at the cucumber sandwich with her fork, lifting it in front of her mouth, staring at it, before lowering it back to her plate. The silverware bounced against the dish with an unsettling clatter.

"Have you lost your appetite, dear?" her mother inquired, reclining back on the nearby loveseat. She reached for her cup and took a sip of tea. "Perhaps the water in the spa was too hot for you?"

"We made certain not to stay in for more than twenty minutes," Ellen pointed out as she flipped the pages of a book on the architecture of Bath purchased at Mr. Godwin's bookshop earlier in the day. "I have heard the heat combined with the pungent mineral odors can make some people queasy."

Camille seized on the excuse to leave, pushing back her chair, and standing up. "I do have a headache. I believe I will go to my bedchamber and rest."

Her mother considered her from lowered brows. "I will come up and check on you later."

Ellen reached out to touch her arm as Camille walked past her. "I am sorry you don't feel well."

"Thank you both for your concern. I am optimistic a nap will set me to rights."

The butler opened the door for her. She strode out of the dining room, across the corridor, and up the stairs. Upon reaching the upper passage, she lifted her skirt above the tops of her slippers and raced to her bedchamber door.

Twisting the doorknob with a shaking hand, the door swung open, and she lunged inside the room. Momentarily gripping the thick plank of wood to steady herself, she swung the door closed behind her, locking it.

She rested her forehead against the smooth surface, shuddering as an image of Frederick's expression came to her once again when she had mistakenly stepped inside the King's Bath a few hours before. There was no doubt he recognized her. She observed his jaw tighten and his eyes narrow with what she hoped was merely a sensation of astonishment. It would be a terrible result of her heedless preoccupation if he had felt scorn or disdain in that moment. Gone would be his offer of assistance. It was also doubtful he would continue to be her friend.

Camille kicked off her slippers and strode across the thick carpet to the bed. With a sigh, she hopped up onto the mattress and flopped onto her back. She starred up at the coffered ceiling, pondering the reason for her distraction that led to a humiliating, awkward outcome.

The outing to visit the Queen's spa began in an untroubled manner. Because of the scanty bathing apparel they wore, her mother insisted that Camille and Ellen cover themselves with a pelisse and each take a chair directly to the spa door. Lady Collins informed them that she and her maid would follow immediately behind them.

Upon arriving at their destination, Camille discovered she had left her bathing cap in her chamber. Her mother arrived moments later. When she explained what had happened, Lady Collins commanded her maid Maud to squire her back to the townhouse to collect the essential adornment.

"I will accompany Miss Cather down to the spa. We will secure seats nearby and wait for your return before going into the water."

A pair of young, enterprising chairman were standing nearby looking for customers. For an additional fare, they were swiftly returned to the Crescent residence, where Camille fetched the cap. They descended back down the hill to the baths in record time.

Mindful that her own carelessness had caused the delay, she surged out of the chair when they reached their destination, calling out to the maid, "I am going down. You may wait for us in the dressing rooms."

Camille marched up to the door and yanked it open. She felt a rush of warm, sulfur-tinged air blow across her face as she peered down through the heavy mist obscuring the stone steps leading down to the bath. She shut the door tightly behind her, tentatively stepping forward. Barely able to ascertain the walkway in the gloom, she reached out to steady herself, grazing the cold, clammy walls with her fingertips. She made her way down with tentative, hesitant movements, until the hard surface gave way to an open room. She became aware of the sounds of lapping water and the murmur of voices. The Queen's Bath must be a few feet away! She surged forward, eager to let her mother know she had returned. Her rushed momentum caused the heated air to billow around her. The heavy mist dissipated, and she could make out the oblong form of the spa just ahead with shadowy images of figures in the water. But something was wrong. She suddenly realized the murmur of voices sounding around her were low and masculine. She froze, the skirts on her gown whirling around her, causing the steam surrounding her to part. That was the moment she spotted Frederick.

"Miss! You have taken the wrong passage! You must not go in there!"

She covered her face with her hands and turned away, silently following the guide back up the stairs and out the door.

Once on the sidewalk, the man took a few long strides to the right to stop in front of an adjoining portal. "This door leads to the Queen's Bath. Observe the Q overhead."

She had charged up the passage, frantically shadowing the guide in a rush to escape. Camille took several deep breathes before turning to back to the door she had entered by mistake. "That looks like a Q as well."

"No, Miss. It is a G for gentlemen."

Camille sat up, swinging her feet off the bed. She stood, crossing her arms over her chest and began pacing back and forth across the plush, carpeted floor. What was wrong with her? She prided herself on her attention to detail in all aspects of her life. She never forgot an engagement and always arrived on time. She kept up a faithful, detailed correspondence with several friends from finishing school. She made certain her gowns were always complemented by tasteful, discreet jewelry, her garments never excessively adorned. Presently, it was hard to remember her name, not to mention important accessories required for bathing in the spa!

The image of Frederick standing in the steamy water would forever be imprinted in her mind. The firm, developed muscles on his chest and arms complimented a lean, tapered waist. He transmitted a perfect combination of strength and attraction in that moment.

Nothing would have been more glorious than to stay and relish the sight of him half naked in the spa. A wave of heat engulfed her body and her legs threatened to buckle underneath her. She reached out to clutch the edge of the mantle.

It was useless to attempt to rest when her thoughts were mired in confusion and lascivious reflections. She would take a short walk. It would clear her mind. Camille rang the bell for Sally.

A knock sounded a few minutes later and the door opened. "Yes, Miss Collins?"

"Come in. I want you to join me for a stroll. There is a nice green space across the street. Go fetch a shawl and meet me in the entry. We will not disturb my mother or Miss Cather."

"Yes, Miss."

When Sally joined her shortly afterward, Camille hastened out the front door with the maid following close behind her. She crossed the street heading to a stand of trees with a bench nearby that she had noticed earlier.

"Camille! Miss Collins!"

She turned to see Frederick striding toward her, and her cheeks suddenly felt scorching hot as if she was standing too close to a roaring fire. "Fred…Lord Surd."

"Are you well?"

"Yes." She put a hand up to her face.

He cleared his throat. "Earlier today, I imagine your maid became confused as to the proper door."

"Stop a moment." Camille looked over her shoulder to see Sally standing a few feet away. "Please wait for me over there on the other side of the hill."

He waited until the woman had disappeared over the rise. "I'm sorry. I spoke without thought to the circumstances."

"No matter." She clutched the ribbons at her neck as a strong breeze tugged at her bonnet. "No one in my household is aware of the unfortunate occurrence that took place. It was all my doing. I am aghast and disconcerted by what happened. You know me well enough to apprehend my exacting ways. I abhor those who draw attention to themselves in society with their foolish, imprudent behavior. I acted in a rash, careless manner, forgetting an essential item necessary to wear while in the spa, requiring the others in my party to wait while I rushed away to retrieve it. Then, upon my return, I compounded my error by charging forward, without due consideration, haphazardly entering a building I had no prior knowledge of. The resulting mortification was well-deserved. I have never been so embarrassed in my life."

Lord Surd reached out to touch her shoulder. "Your reaction is too severe. You are residing in a new environment. To my knowledge, you have never lived anywhere other than your brother's country estate and his townhouse in London. It is not uncommon for someone in those circumstances to take a few days to familiarize themselves to novel surroundings."

"You are too gracious, my lord. I thank you for attempting to sooth what you clearly imagine are my bruised sensibilities and appreciate your gallant attempt to excuse my disconcerting behavior." She took a deep breath. "I have resolved to temper myself from this day forward and face new challenges or circumstances with the utmost composure and tranquility."

"Are you saying you will no longer be the spirited, lively young woman, enthusiastically participating in your daily activities who often provides me with refreshingly candid observations about her experiences?"

Camille's cheeks grew warm again at his choice of words. "Yes. That is correct. Undoubtedly you will have reason to be grateful for my decision before many days have passed."

"Why would you believe I should find your resolution comforting?"

An image of reticent, gracious Mrs. Hervey as she smiled at Frederick appeared before her. "I apprehend gentlemen prefer ladies who conduct themselves with a quiet, gentle dignity. I must learn from their example and moderate my conduct."

He rubbed his forehead with one gloved hand, studying her. "You speak of other gentlemen. You must know that you are not describing my preferences."

"Miss Collins! We should return!" the maid called out, from the top of the rise. "Your mother will be worried if she discovers you are not in your room."

"Yes. A moment, Sally." Camille turned back. "Perhaps you have not fully realized what your inclinations and propensities are. I am confident all my acquaintances will be agreeably influenced by the adjustments I intend to make to my character and disposition."

He took a few steps forward, reaching out to clasp her hands in a firm grip. "Please remember what I am about to say, Camille. I have never, ever had cause to desire a change in your aspect or temperament. I bid you a good evening."

She watched Frederick walk away from her, knowing she would always remember those words just as she would continually recall the image of the cascade of water running down across his broad chest and muscular arms as he stared at her from inside the King's spa earlier that day.

Chapter Eleven

Frederick speared the last bit of egg with his fork before dropping the utensil onto his plate and taking a sip of coffee. He stared out of the window, studying the surrounding landscape. The sky was clear of clouds, bright sunlight was already covering the tops of many of the taller trees. It promised to be one of those rare, warm late September days. The sound of someone clearing their throat made him turn around. His uncle's butler stood in the doorway.

"Yes, Rigsby?"

"Excuse me, my lord. I'm sorry to bother you at breakfast. You have two visitors. Shall I tell them you are not at home?"

"To see me? I wasn't expecting anyone. I have finished." He stood up, pushing his chair back underneath the table. "Who is it?"

Rigsby pursed his lips together before replying. "A Mr. Heaviside and a Mr. Marshall. I believe they are known as the Masters of Ceremonies."

"Masters of Ceremonies?" He chuckled. "It would certainly be a slap in the face to send such important personages on their way without favoring them with an interview. I will see the gentlemen."

"Very good, my lord. I have placed them in the drawing room."

"Thank you, Rigsby." He followed the butler out of

the dining room and strode up the stairs. The drawing room door was open. He walked inside. Two men sat on the edge of the two chairs flanking the fireplace. They came to their feet simultaneously when he crossed the threshold and bowed to him. "I am Lord Surd. You wished to speak to me?"

"A pleasure, my lord!" gushed a portly man, well past his youth. He reached up to tug at the edges of a plain stock that wrapped around his burly neck. The front of his shirt was decorated in the old-fashioned manner with a frill of lace, drooping over the upper edge of his waistcoat. A dark green satin ribbon with a gold medallion edged with blue enamel, set round with brilliant stones, dangled at its end, across his broad chest. The medallion had a raised figure of what appeared to be the goddess Venus in the center. This showy badge lay against his garish, purple waistcoat. He wore dark grey knee-breeches, matching silk stockings and black leather pumps adorned with oversized, silver buckles on his feet. "I am Mr. James Heaviside, Master of Ceremonies for the Upper Rooms. I received your application for a subscription. I felt it prudent to come and make your acquaintance without delay. If you are not already aware, the first dress ball of the season is Monday night."

"I had no knowledge of the event. Thank you for informing me, Mr. Heaviside. I would certainly like to attend the ball."

"I am happy to make your acquaintance as well, my lord." The other man stepped forward. Tall and thin, not much beyond middle age, he wore more restrained clothing without lace and harsh colors; a dark blue wool coat supplemented with matching trousers and black leather pumps. A satin ribbon in a green hue more discreet than Mr. Heaviside's, was wrapped around his neck with a silver badge hanging on the end. It featured a wreath of laurel embossed on the front. "My name is Mr. Charles H. Marshall. I oversee interviewing and accepting those who wish to patronize the Lower Rooms."

"It is good to meet you both. Please sit down." He took a chair facing the men as they settled themselves. "I must admit, this is my first visit to Bath. I am woefully ignorant of the rules for attending the assemblies."

"It is an honor to welcome you, my lord. Do you reside in London?" asked Mr. Heaviside.

"Yes. The metropolis is my primary residence. I spend time at my family's estate near Maidenhead, Berkshire as well."

"What brings you to Bath, my lord?" inquired Mr. Marshall.

"My uncle, Mr. Leonard Melter, is here taking the waters in hopes of improving his health. I am keeping him company for a time."

"Ah, yes! I called here soon after Mr. Melter arrived in town," acknowledged Mr. Heaviside. "He informed me he believed he would have no occasion to visit the upper or lower rooms because of discomfort and hindrance brought on by gout. I trust the waters have provided him with some relief?"

"Thank you for inquiring. I believe there has been improvement in his condition."

"I am gratified to hear that, my lord. As to the rules, now that the season has begun, the Upper Rooms will hold a Dress Ball on Monday nights and a Fancy Ball on Thursday evening. The attendees are requested to assemble as soon as possible after six o'clock. The balls will end precisely at eleven, even if this means stopping in the middle of a dance."

"I see. May I ask what the difference is between a Dress and a Fancy Ball?"

Mr. Heaviside cleared his throat while fingering his badge. "Dress Balls feature formal, set attire. Gentlemen are required to wear breeches and must not wear half-boots or riding boots in the ballroom. Ladies may not wear hats. Hoops under their gowns and lappets in their hair are required when dancing the minuets. Normally, they are performed by two dancers but ours are done in sets of three couples, to accommodate the large groups of people who attend these events. We also offer country dances during the final half of the session. The Fancy Balls are a more relaxed affair, the cotillion is danced then. The men may wear trousers or pantaloons and the women may leave off the hoops and lappets at those events. Many come in costume."

"I wish to point out, my lord, my rooms hold Dress Balls on Fridays and Fancy Balls on Tuesdays. The dress etiquette is the same, but the balls start at eight o'clock and end at precisely midnight," clarified Mr. Marshall. "The Lower Rooms also offer sweeping views of the River Avon, and vistas of green meadows flanked by wooded hills from the windows of the ballroom. We serve breakfast there, and on the outdoor terrace on warm days, for those who make early morning visits to the Pump Room for a glass of water or a dip in the spas. There are convenient stone walkways surrounding the building where the visitors may enjoy a delightful promenade as well."

"The Upper Rooms offer a tearoom and a card room, though I wish to make known to you, my lord, no Hazard or other unlawful games are allowed on any account whatsoever, nor is card playing permitted in the rooms on Sundays," added Mr. Heaviside, with hearty resoluteness. "The dances are halted midway through the evening so that the couples may enjoy wine and tea. We also offer concerts on Wednesday evenings and lectures at one o'clock on Monday, Wednesday, and Friday. Talks on Egypt's history and its antiquities are scheduled for next week. Violin lessons will be given later in the month as well."

"I must admit, I had no notion of the extensive array of entertainment and educational choices Bath had to offer."

Mr. Heaviside chuckled, and then started to wheeze. He reached for his handkerchief and coughed into it. "I assure you, my lord, Bath provides amusements similar to the excellent quality you are familiar with in the fine city of London."

"Indeed," concurred Mr. Marshall. "May I also recommend seeing a play in our newly refurbished Theatre Royal? Guy Manning will be performed there next Saturday evening."

Frederick came to his feet, suddenly eager to be outside relishing the warm sunshine. "Thank you, gentlemen, for your information and suggestions. How is the payment for the dances, concerts, lectures, refreshments, and use of the card room to be handled?"

"For how long you plan to visit the city, my lord?"

"Possibly a month."

"Half a guinea to each of us will cover the subscriptions and fees for the amusements and use of the rooms during that time, my lord."

Payments to each of the gentlemen were quickly

handled and concluded to all parties' satisfaction. Rigsby was summoned to escort them to the door while Frederick went to his bedchamber to collect his coat from his valet. Minutes later, he was striding down the front steps of the townhouse, making his way to Milsom Street.

He determined to visit the Pump Room first to see if he could locate Mr. Vane. Because of the other occupants in the King's spa, as well as his uncle, there hadn't been an opportunity to discuss Camille's awkward, fleeting appearance with him yesterday. He was almost certain Mr. Vane had recognized her. Frederick wanted to comprehend there was no chance he would mention her unfortunate mistake to others.

He had almost reached the corner of Milsom and Quiet Streets when he spied Mrs. Hervey walking out of the front door of her residence.

"Good morning!" he called out to her.

She came to a sudden stop, twisting around to face him. "Oh! Good day, Lord Surd!"

"Are you heading to visit the Pump Room? May I escort you there?"

"Yes. However, I don't intend to remain there long. It is such a lovely day. I thought to take a stroll on the Terrace Walk in front of the Lower Rooms."

He chuckled as he offered her his arm. "You will be surprised to learn I am familiar with the location. A few minutes ago, I concluded an introductory meeting with two of Bath's most illustrious gentlemen. The Masters of Ceremonies, Mr. Heaviside, and Mr. Marshall."

She smiled. "Gracious! Both men at once? A great honor has indeed been bestowed upon you."

"I admit I was surprised by the number of

amusements offered here," he acknowledged with a grin. "Are you aware there is to be a dress ball on Monday evening at the Upper Rooms?"

"Yes. I believe the Upper and Lower Rooms each hold two balls weekly on different nights during the season."

"May I request a dance from you?"

"Oh! No, my lord. I rarely go out in the evening. I do not have a companion who could accompany me. I sometimes attend the lectures in the afternoons."

"I am sorry you will not attend the ball." He led her across Cheap Street toward the Pump Room entrance when he suddenly spied Mr. Vane walking away from him down the road toward the river. "Excuse me, I must have a word with someone."

"Go on about your business. I am perfectly able to see myself inside."

"I will be with you momentarily," he promised and turned away, striding down the street. "Mr. Vane!"

The gentleman halted his forward movement and turned around to face him with one brow raised. He bowed. "Lord Surd."

"I apologize for coming upon you so suddenly. There was no chance to speak to you after the incident."

He studied him intently. "You refer to the matter of the woman entering the wrong spa yesterday?"

"Yes." Frederick realized no name had been mentioned. "Are you aware of her identity?"

"I am. If you are concerned that I will tell the tale, bandy her name about to the others and make her a laughingstock, you may immediately cease all apprehension of my doing so. She made an understandable error. The doorways are poorly marked.

Recall I spoke yesterday of my intention to look about me for a wife. I believe Miss Collins would suit me quite well."

"Oomph!" Frederick's gut wrenched as if he had been hit with a punishing left hook.

Mr. Vane frowned as he reached out toward him. "Are you well?"

"Yes…Yes." He gulped and then swallowed some of the fresh morning air.

"If you are certain?" Mr. Vane contemplated him for a moment before taking a step away. "Excuse me. I promised my sister to bring some of Sally Lunn's acclaimed buns back for tea. Miss Collins and Miss Cather have consented to visit her again this morning."

"Don't let me take up any more of your time. Please, carry on." When he had gone, Frederick stood staring down at the ground, attempting to compose himself. His thoughts refused to settle, racing like a spooked stallion around and around in his head. It had been his understanding, when Camille refused his offer of marriage, it was a temporary postponement. Surely, she hadn't meant she would never, ever consider his suit? He shook his head with exasperation, telling himself to ignore his sense of unease. Mr. Vane and Camille had only recently become acquainted. The man was at least twenty-five years older than her as well. It was irrational to become alarmed by Mr. Vane's intentions. For his own piece of mind, he must continue to think of it as simply an ambiguous hope or notion.

He took a deep breath, retracing his steps back to the Pump Room and came upon Mrs. Hervey standing just inside the doorway taking a final sip of her water.

She wrinkled her nose as she placed the empty glass

on the tray. "I keep hoping the taste will improve."

Frederick forced his lips to curve into a semblance of a smile, recalling his companion had played no role in the predicament he currently faced with Camille. It was hardly productive to be blue-deviled while in her company. "I believe it is said, '*a thing that is truly repugnant can never be augmented for the better.*'"

She raised her fine, shapely brows. "Wise words. Who said them?"

He chuckled, offering her his arm. "I don't recall. Shall we stroll down to the Terrace Walk?"

She held back. "Are you not going to partake of your daily dose of water?"

He scowled. "I believe no harm will come to me if I decline the pleasure for today."

She laughed. "Don't let the Masters of Ceremonies hear of your decision. They would be forced to temper their appropriation of your presence in the city."

"I will make certain word of my unruly behavior never reaches their ears," he vowed, as they walked past the Bath Abbey toward the South Parade.

"A beautiful edifice," Mrs. Hervey observed as she paused in front of the building's massive front entrance. "It's too lovely a day to spend indoors. When the weather is cooler, you should view the interior. I try to attend the services at noon every Sunday. The organ music is a wondrous addition when singing the hymns."

"I certainly will make a point to see the inside," Frederick promised. They stepped out onto York Street. He could see the River Avon just ahead. The street suddenly widened. Several groups of people were strolling on smooth, golden sandstone walkways in front of them. To the right, a raised platform jutted out in front of a substantial building. It contained tables and chairs placed in front of open glass doors leading to a large interior room with a high ceiling, decorated in the center with two elegant chandeliers. A few servants were carrying trays containing teapots, cups and tiny plates of sweets or sandwiches to the customers sitting at the tables. He suddenly had a notion. He would question Mrs. Hervey about her own courtship and betrothal. Perhaps her experience could provide him with a clue on how to proceed with Camille. He determined it would be preferable to take a seat in order to better observe Mrs. Hervey's facial expressions when she replied to his queries. He placed his free hand on top of hers. "I have a favor to ask of you. Could you tell me about your courtship before you agreed to marry Mr. Hervey? Shall we sit and have a spot of tea, while we pretend to watch the crowds mill around in front of us?"

She gripped his arm and her brown eyes widened. "There isn't much to disclose."

He patted her hand. "Nevertheless, I am certain I would benefit greatly from your revelations. I require nothing of a personal nature, just a description of the general manner with which the suit was conducted."

Mrs. Hervey studied him. "May I ask why you need to know this information?"

He glanced at a group of children playing catch nearby, giving himself a moment to decide upon an appropriate explanation without revealing too much. "I have a friend in London who recently had a lady turn him down after informing her of his intention to pay his addresses to her. I thought to give him some advice on how to proceed and secure the lady's interest."

She frowned. "Were the couple well-acquainted or

had the two of them only recently been introduced?"

"They met by chance several years ago. I…They have a close relationship."

"It is surprising she refused him if they are devoted to one another. Very well. I will answer your queries, but I warn you, my own experience could be described as mundane at best."

They made their way to one of the empty tables on the far side of the platform. Once Mrs. Hervey settled herself and he had taken the chair opposite her, Frederick ordered a pot of tea and a plate of sugar biscuits the waiter recommended. "I believe you mentioned previously you met your husband at a ball in London?"

"Yes, while he was on leave for an injury he had sustained during the war with France."

"Were you immediately attracted to him?"

She studied her gloved hands. "I remember thinking he was certainly quite handsome when we were first introduced by a mutual acquaintance. I felt grateful when he requested a dance with me."

"Grateful?" Frederick raised his brows. "I am surprised by your word choice."

She looked directly at him, her gaze intent on his face. "By now, you have surely discovered I am a timid person. I attended a few balls in London. While there, usually spending the evening sitting on a chair watching the others dance, I was gratified to receive notice from an attractive gentleman."

"Was the first dance you had with him memorable?" he prodded.

Her pale cheeks flushed a bright pink. "I suppose you could say it was noteworthy. He stepped on the train and ripped my gown."

"You proceeded to the ladies' retiring room to have your garment repaired and never saw Mr. Hervey again that evening?" He nodded to the waiter as he placed the tea and biscuits on the table.

"Nothing so straightforward." She cringed as she reached for the teapot, pouring the hot beverage into their cups, and handing one to Frederick. "When he stepped on the edge of the fabric, I had already moved forward to complete the dance pattern around the opposite partner. The tugging and pulling on my gown caused the seam underneath my bodice to split open. I was completely exposed."

The spoon he picked up to stir in milk and sugar fell from his fingers, dropping with a loud clang onto the saucer. "I am sorry. You needn't provide me with any further details."

She lowered the teapot back to the table and cleared her throat. "You indicated you wished to gain knowledge about obtaining a woman's regard. In my case, the gratification that I told you I felt initially, increased tenfold when Thomas immediately offered his assistance with no hint of uncertainty or reluctance on his part. He whisked off his coat and wrapped me up securely in the garment before the guests scarcely had an opportunity to register what happened. I fell in love with him in that moment."

Chapter Twelve

"I believe I see Mrs. Hervey and Lord Surd sitting at one of the tables on the terrace," remarked Ellen. "Should we stroll over and greet them?"

Camille looked in the direction of the outdoor seating area at the Lower Rooms, quickly spotting them. They were staring intently at one another, deep in conversation. "No, no. I have a hunch they would not welcome our company at the present time."

"It appears Lord Surd is enchanted with the lady," Ellen observed. "Upon reflection, it is not surprising."

"Indeed?" Her comment caused Camille's heart to beat erratically inside her chest. She took several deep breaths before speaking. "I would appreciate if you would clarify why the situation is predictable."

"You know what the gossips say. Young men often choose lonely widows in order to further their experience before marriage."

"Experience?" Her face felt hot and flushed. "You don't mean…?"

"Camille! Ellen! Isn't the weather glorious? I find it hard to believe it will be the first of October the day after tomorrow."

Camille turned to see her mother accompanied by her friend strolling toward them. "Mother, Mrs. Warwick. It is indeed uncommonly warm."

"Your skin tone is quite red, my dear," her mother

observed. "You have been out in the sun too long."

"I see an unoccupied bench in the shade. Perhaps we should sit there for a short period?" suggested Mrs. Warwick.

Ellen took a step closer, clutching Camille's arm and whispering in her ear, "I apologize for speaking of such matters. I never intended to discompose you. I believed the practice was commonly known if not often acknowledged."

"Please do not fret. I am aware of the convention," Camille murmured as she forced her feet to move in the direction of the empty seat. "I simply hadn't connected the tradition with Lord Surd. That is all."

She sat down, reclining against the back of the bench with a sigh, careful to keep her gaze averted away from the terrace. Her mother informed her that she and Ellen would walk down to the river while she reposed herself on the bench. Mrs. Warwick took a seat next to her.

"I understand you and Miss Cather are planning to attend the dress ball Monday night."

"Yes. Yes, we are."

Mrs. Warwick bent toward her, speaking softly. "Are you aware of the requirement of hoops and lappets for the ladies?"

"Hoops and lappets?" Camille frowned. "No one mentioned the obligation to me."

The other lady sighed. "I imagine Mr. Heaviside and Mr. Marshall were hesitant to discuss such a topic with young ladies or perhaps they assumed you were aware of the rules. Your mother told me the Masters of Ceremonies had come by to introduce themselves."

"Yes. We met them both yesterday. They made a

mention of the various amusements and entertainments to be experienced at each of their rooms and clarified which days of the week the events could be experienced. However, I recall no mention of imperative adornments for the balls."

"No matter. I am confident I can assist you." Mrs. Warwick glanced up. "Here come the others now."

Miss Warwick and Miss Talbot strolled toward them with Mr. Warwick ambling along behind. The ladies were brilliantly attired in walking dresses in similar shades of primrose yellow with matching silk pelisses. They each wore low-crowned straw bonnets on their heads with broad rims partially obscuring their eyes. Miss Talbot twirled an open parasol over her head with one hand. Miss Warwick's gloved fingers clutched Miss Talbot's arm as she giggled at a whispered comment made by her companion. Mr. Warwick sported a wooden cane adorned with a gleaming silver cap. He rested it upon one shoulder, like a piece of timber. His corpulent frame was covered by a pea green coat decorated with large, garish gold buttons. A lavishly tied cravat surrounded his burly throat and his thighs were covered in chocolate brown breeches, fastened at the knees with flamboyant buckles that glittered in the bright sunlight.

"My dears." Mrs. Warwick smiled warmly at the group. "I was discussing the upcoming dress ball with Miss Collins. Here are Lady Collins and Miss Cather."

"It is much cooler by the water, Camille," her mother remarked, as she and Ellen joined them.

"I am much improved after sitting in the shade," Camille informed her, while giving Ellen a pointed look.

"I spoke with your daughter, Margaret," disclosed Mrs. Warwick. "I was dismayed to learn the Masters of

Ceremonies failed to inform you of the necessity to wear certain embellishments Monday evening."

"Embellishments?" Lady Collins raised her brows. "To what do you refer?"

"So droll!" Miss Warwick twittered. "The ladies are required to attend any dress balls given in Bath attired in gowns with panniers or hoops underneath and one's hair must be ornamented with lace lappets."

"How utterly diverting!" pronounced Miss Talbot in a boisterous manner. "We are to mimic our Georgian ancestors! I have no doubt we ladies are required to don caps over our hair and the gentlemen must come attired in breeches as well."

"With long coats, ornamented by large, resplendent buttons," interjected Mr. Warwick, with an exuberant, rapturous expression on his face.

"Additionally, if one wishes to dance, the minuet is all that is allowed for the first half of the session," added Miss Warwick with a scowl.

"La! What tales you tell, cousin!" snickered Miss Talbot.

"I assure you, Priscilla, your cousin is speaking the truth," admonished Mrs. Warwick. "I believe it is a way to honor Bath's zenith in the last century."

"Currently in London, hoops are worn for court presentations only," Lady Collins pointed out.

"If this is true, how are we to obtain proper gowns to wear at Monday night's ball?" Ellen queried with a frown.

"I was about to explain the means to accomplish that," Mrs. Warwick responded, favoring all of them with a smug smile. "Anticipating my daughter would need to have a variety of gowns in this style handy to wear to the balls, I had a local modiste create several for her last year, along with some panniers. You ladies are much alike in size. The gowns would require a minimum of adjustment to make them fit. I'm certain you will agree to this notion, Honora?"

"I hadn't thought…" She stopped mid-sentence as her mother glared at her. "Of course."

"I also have two gowns and hoops that should fit you, Margaret." Mrs. Warwick smiled warmly at Camille's mother.

"Are you certain?" Lady Collins grimaced, looking down at her herself and then glancing at her slender friend.

"No need to fret, my dear," she replied. "You recall my widowed sister-in-law resided with us until her passing a few years ago? I am certain her gowns will fit you."

"You must all come to tea this afternoon and try on the garments," Mrs. Warwick entreated. "Honora's lady's maid is quite handy with a needle. She can quickly make any required adjustments. Does this proposition meet with everyone's approval?"

"I'm certain neither my daughter nor Miss Cather brought gowns that would be appropriate," Lady Collins remarked with a lift of her brows as she considered Camille.

"You are correct, Mother, we did not."

"The prevailing favored style of ball gowns wouldn't provide enough space to wear panniers underneath the garments we transported here, in any case," clarified Ellen.

"Thankfully not," agreed Miss Talbot, with a disdainful sniff. "I suppose I must agree to participate in this absurd diversion. It would never do to sit in my bedchamber with a book all evening."

"I will attend with pleasure." Camille spoke in a strident tone, in order to be heard over Miss Talbot's persistent grumbles.

"A diversion not to be missed? Please, describe this admirable event to me." Lord Surd commented from behind her.

At the sound of his resonant, affable voice, Camille twisted around to face him. He stood grinning at her, his wide brown eyes shimmering like smoldering embers in a well-banked fire. She raised a shaking hand to her cheek, tucking a stray lock of hair back behind one ear. "Fr...Lord Surd. We were discussing the dress ball which is to take place Monday evening in the Upper Rooms."

He bowed and then moved forward to join their group. "Miss Talbot gave the impression the diversion was beneath her notice," he pointed out.

"Apparently the ladies are required to wear outmoded, unfashionable gowns and sport lappets in their hair," clarified Ellen. "Does Mrs. Hervey plan to go?"

"No, she does not." He frowned. "Mrs. Hervey assured me her lack of interest in attending the ball was of no consequence since she is of a demure nature. I sense she is a lonely woman at heart, though she would never admit such a thing to me."

"Lord Surd, I don't believe you have been introduced to Mrs. Warwick," Lady Collins reached for her friend's arm and guided her forward. "We have known each other since we were children."

"Mrs. Warwick." He bowed. "Delighted. Do you

reside here in Bath year-round?"

She curtsied to him. "A pleasure, Lord Surd. Yes, we do. I believe you have already met my son, daughter, and niece? Upon my husband's passing seven years ago, our townhouse in London was sold. My children and I settled here in the house that has been passed to the oldest son in my husband's family for several generations. Will you grace the upper rooms with your presence on Monday night, my lord?"

"I certainly plan to make an appearance."

Mr. Warwick made his way to the front of their group with an exaggerated, mincing step. He bowed low, placing his cane at his side. His pudgy fingers gripped the silver ornament on its tip as he stood straight once more. "Lord Surd, I trust you packed a pair of breeches in your traveling bag to wear to the ball? I recall they are required attire for all gentlemen frequenting Almack's in London during the season."

Lord Surd's brows rose as his intent gaze swept over Mr. Warwick's ostentatious garments. "As I matter of fact, I did. May I inquire, who is your tailor?"

Mr. Warwick stretched his stocky neck and pointed his nose in the air, presumably taking the opportunity to provide a peer of the realm an optimum view of his ensemble. "I am gratified you recognize a true master of fashion, my lord. Mr. Sculthorpe is my man, on Broad Street."

"Certainly, true satisfaction with one's appearance depends entirely on taste and their definition of style," Frederick whispered with a chuckle into Camille's ear.

"If we wish to attend the ball, we must make certain the ladies have an appropriate gown to wear," Mrs. Warwick reminded them. "I apologize, Lord Surd, we must bid you farewell. The time is quite short to accomplish so much."

"I understand. I look forward to seeing all of you there," he replied before reaching out to grasp Camille's arm as she made to slip by him. "Before you leave, I wish to request a dance Monday evening."

In that moment, the anxious, resentful sensations Camille experienced whenever she observed Frederick keeping company with Mrs. Hervey reached a boiling point. Her body trembled and there was a tight, constricting pressure in her chest, which affected her ability to breathe. She suddenly wanted to inflict a modicum of distress upon him. She kept her gaze trained on his hand, not wishing to observe the disillusionment she was certain would be reflected in his eyes. "I must decline your petition, Lord Surd. I have no wish to dance with you."

Chapter Thirteen

Frederick pulled absentmindedly at the lace on the edge of his sleeves as he stood inside the doorway that led to the ballroom. Thankfully, his uncle had loaned him one of his shirts embellished in the old style with a goffered lace frill at the neck and wrists, a plain stock, as well as a long, cut away coat in Corbeau green to wear with his breeches. His shins were covered with white cotton stockings, and he wore black pumps decorated with small, silver buckles on his feet.

After hearing Camille's outright rejection of his request for a dance with her, Frederick had pondered rescinding his stated intention to attend the ball. But upon reflection, he determined such an action would be cowardly as well as uncivil.

The first minuet of the evening was in progress. He strolled inside the room, noting the high ceiling and the five gleaming chandeliers dangling from it. The walls were decorated with fluted Corinthian columns, complimented with friezes depicting Greek keys alternating with elegant images of lilies. He turned to his left, making his way to the rear of a cluster of seated, elderly matrons who were busy gossiping about the young ladies' gowns. Several mature gentlemen stood behind their chairs discussing politics. He unobtrusively joined their group, intending to observe the others on the dance floor without attracting undue attention to himself.

Frederick spotted Miss Talbot first. She blithely executed the dance steps upon the ballroom floor close to his location. Clad in a pistachio-green robe over a matching petticoat and stomacher, decorated profusely with tiny bows, she laughed boisterously at a comment her partner made to her as they bowed and curtsied to one another, crossed the floor and traded sides. It appeared she had overcome her earlier blatant distress over attending the evening's entertainment.

As the dancers changed positions, other couples came into view. He noted Miss Warwick attired in a fawn-colored robe partially covering a light brown stomacher and petticoat. She was partnered by her brother, brazenly pretentious in a deep purple coat, stripped Bishop's blue waistcoat and black breeches fastened with a glistening silver button just below his thickset knees.

The dancers switched sides and Frederick's heart squeezed painfully inside his chest when he saw Camille. Her gown was of a light Pomona-green, a perfect foil for her dark hair and dazzling, emerald eyes. Her glorious ebony hair was gathered into a frilly lace cap perched on the crown of her head. She danced with Mr. Vane, who was attired sedately in an unadorned biscuit-colored coat, covering a plain, dark-brown waistcoat and black breeches.

He studied Camille covertly as she made to cross the floor, pirouetting around her partner, her expression somber and resigned. Mr. Vane spoke softly to her as they passed each other. She moved her head to one side, causing the lace lappets dangling from her cap to flutter enticingly against her exposed neck.

"Lord Surd, welcome. Do you intend to dance?"

Frederick turned to see the Master of Ceremonies, Mr. Heaviside, standing at his side. Resplendent in a bottle green coat over a puce-colored waistcoat, the gold medallion gleaming prominently against his chest, suspended from his stout neck by the green, satin ribbon. "Good evening, sir. I have just arrived and was contemplating the others."

The older man indicated the crowded ballroom with a sweep of his bulky hand. "Do not hesitate too long to choose your partner, my lord. There is only one more minuet before I stop the dancing briefly for tea."

"Lord Surd, please come join us," Lady Collins stepped forward, placing her hand on his arm. "We have secured a place at the other side of the room."

"Very well."

Lady Collins led him around the edge of the dance floor to a spot directly across from the musicians' gallery. She released his arm to join Mrs. Warwick, who was standing near the wall, murmuring to her daughter. Her son sauntered up to them, fiddling with a button on his coat. Frederick's attention was drawn to a young lady sitting in a wheeled chair nearby.

Mr. Vane suddenly appeared at his side. "I don't believe you have met my sister. I have introduced her to the others." "Miss Julianna Vane. Julianna, this is Lord Surd."

"I am honored to meet you, my lord," she told him, holding out one gloved hand to him, with a warm smile. "I am celebrating my birthday tonight!"

"Miss Vane. I wish you many happy returns." He gently clasped her fingers before releasing them and bowing. She was painfully thin. He noted the pinched, sunken cheekbones.

Her drowsy, opaque eyes studied him in turn. "Thank you, my lord. My brother has spoken of you, but he failed to provide an accurate description. I promised him I would not dance tonight but beholding you with your handsome visage and elegant attire, makes me wish to rescind my vow."

"Julianna!" Mr. Vane growled her name between tense, stretched lips.

She sighed. "It was only a momentary yearning, Harcourt. A wish to be myself once more. I know it is not possible yet. Do you have a partner for the next minuet, Lord Surd? It would bring me great pleasure to watch you dance."

"No, I do not. I had intended…"

Miss Vane twisted around in her chair. "Miss Collins, there you are! Come away from the wall and join us."

Frederick looked up to see Camille walking with hesitant steps toward them. He swiftly turned away to find Miss Cather standing close behind him, speaking with Miss Talbot. "Miss Cather, will you partner me in the minuet?"

She started with surprise, glancing over his shoulder with her brows raised, before facing him and curtsying. "Yes. Of course, Lord Surd."

Frederick offered his gloved left hand to her, and she placed her right one on top of his. They turned and made their way to the dance floor, taking their places at one end, facing the assembled company. Two other couples joined them, one pair moving to the opposite end of the floor, the other two to the center. He tapped down a sudden surge of nervousness as he scanned the crowd of eager onlookers. There were few occasions in the past when he had been obligated to perform the minuet. He mentally reviewed the steps he learned as a youth from his dance master, grateful that the customary single-couple dance had been altered in Bath to accommodate several couples at the same time.

The musicians began to play. He and Miss Cather turned to confront each other. He bowed to her, and she curtsied. They reached out in unison to momentarily touch gloved hands. With the heels of their shoes lifted off the floor, they pirouetted away from each other, stepping lightly on their toes, allowing their ankles to assume control of the movements as they bobbed and weaved across the hard surface. Now, it was time to move into the Z portion of the dance. Two steps to the left, two steps forward. Frederick remembered to look directly at his partner as she passed on his right side to step back and face one another once more. This was repeated for six more turns. The music came to a stop just as they retreated to their original position on the dance floor.

Frederick bowed deeply to Miss Cather as she curtsied to him. He became aware of the sound of clapping hands as he stood straight once more, blinking with confusion.

"That was glorious, Lord Surd and Miss Cather! I have never enjoyed watching a minuet so much! It was performed so regally!" enthused Miss Vane, her hands clasped in front of her as she sat stiff and straight in her push chair.

Miss Cather blushed. "I am happy my amateur attempt at dancing the minuet has brought you such pleasure."

"Never say so!" Miss Vane entreated. "You carried

yourself so majestically, your steps undeviating and rhythmic! Lord Surd, you were resplendent, magnificent!"

He chuckled as he bowed low over her outstretched hand. "Thank you for your kind words, Miss Vane. It has been many years. I can only say I am grateful my dance master is not present to refute your words of praise."

"Ladies and Gentlemen! Your attention, please!" called out Mr. Heaviside as he stood in the entranceway. "We will now take a pause in the entertainment. Some refreshments are provided in the tearoom. The country dances begin in thirty minutes' time. Remember, we stop immediately at the stroke of eleven o'clock."

Miss Talbot stepped forward, directly in front of Frederick. She released a gusty sigh. "Thank goodness! We may at last remove these awkward hoops! Come, Honora! You as well, Miss Cather. We don't want to miss any of the dancing."

Lady Collins strolled up to him. "Lord Surd, may I trouble you to escort me into the tearoom?"

He put out his arm. "With pleasure, my lady."

"What is your initial impression of Bath, my lord?" she inquired as they walked out of the ballroom.

"I have been pleasantly surprised by the ample assortment of amusements to be had as well as the diverse selection of shops to choose from."

"I have not visited Bath for many years. I was last here as a young bride. The city experienced its zenith in popularity at that time. Certainly, many came here initially for the health benefits touted from drinking or bathing in the spa water, but now other towns have found favor with those seeking cures for illnesses. It has changed substantially but I believe for the better. The excessive crowds made a city of this size quite oppressive. I believe Bath is more restful and pleasant without the confluence of people flocking here."

"It is hard for me to imagine truly appreciating this beautiful city if I were forced to experience it alongside crowds of others who visited without interest in its architecture or pleasing situation on the banks of River Avon, rather simply because it was society's expectation."

"Endeavor to picture the steep, narrow streets of Bath jammed with sedan chairs, each containing their own garishly costumed gentleman or excessively jeweled and embellished lady, all heading for the same location, intent on making their own grand entrance to an assembly room that was already crowded with others determined to accomplish the same triumph. That was the city when I first visited."

"Pardon me, Lady Collins. Lord Surd, Julianna has a favor to ask of you," Mr. Vane's gruff voice sounded in his ear.

Frederick turned to face Mr. Vane. Camille stood beside him, her gloved hand clutching his forearm. Miss Vane reclined next to them in her push chair.

Miss Vane grinned at him. "Since the weather continues to be quite warm, my brother has graciously agreed to allow me to invite a few of our acquaintances to partake of a picnic lunch on the grass in front of our residence in The Circus on Wednesday afternoon. Will you please join us, my lord?"

"I am sorry. I must decline your invitation." He remembered Mrs. Hervey's reference to the weekly lectures and pondered the schedule Mr. Heaviside had recited to him earlier that day, trusting he remembered the correct information. "I made plans to attend a lecture on Egypt's history and antiquities on Wednesday."

Miss Vane frowned, studying her clasped hands. Suddenly, her expression brightened, and she faced him with a wide smile. "I recall the lectures are also offered on Friday afternoons. You may come to my picnic and attend the talks later in the week."

He glanced at Camille before he answered. A stiff, inscrutable expression shrouded her face. "I am engaged to attend the lecture with an acquaintance. It would be ungracious to back out of my prior commitment."

"You are welcome to bring your friend as well."

"Julianna! You grow too forceful with your entreaties," admonished her brother. He stepped forward and placed his hands on the bar at the back of her chair. "You must be tired. We will return home now. Please take your leave of the others."

"Very well. It was good of you to allow me to observe the dancing this evening, Harcourt." Miss Vane sighed. "Good-bye Lady Collins, Lord Surd, and Miss Collins. I expect to see all who are not otherwise engaged at my picnic on Wednesday."

Mr. Vane murmured something to Camille before he turned the push chair around and headed toward the door.

"Will you join us and have a cup of tea before the dancing begins once more, Lord Surd?" inquired Lady Collins, as she glanced at her daughter. "You will both find it hard to concentrate on the steps if you are parched."

"Mother, I don't think…"

"I am sorry," Frederick hastily uttered the words and bowed. "My uncle's gout has been causing him great discomfort. I promised to return this evening to keep him company after the first part of the program was over. You must excuse me."

He turned away, striding out of the tearoom to the octagon-shaped ante chamber and down the corridor to the vestibule.

"Lord Surd!"

He swiveled around to see Camille rushing toward him.

"Cam…Miss Collins! What has happened?" He held his arms out to her as she surged forward.

She gripped his gloved fingers and took a deep breath, releasing it in shaky, gulping gasps. "I…I want to apologize for my churlish behavior, for the spiteful words I said to you. You have a right to question why such a thing has come to pass. I am ashamed to say I do not know the reason. You know me well. There is no need to describe to you my penchant for blunt, plain-speaking. However, only days ago, I apologized for speaking out of turn, inadvertently causing Mrs. Hervey grief. I had determined to handle any subsequent awkward social situations with decorum and consideration and vowed to never speak without first making appropriate consideration of my comments."

He took a moment to admire Camille's flushed, rosy cheeks and her thick, curly dark brown locks. A few of the strands had escaped from her lacy cap, twisting enticingly against one downy earlobe. Her glorious, radiant emerald-green eyes were targeted upon his face. And her sweet, button nose perched above those prim, bow-shaped lips! He clenched his teeth together, admonishing himself to resist the fervent urge to bend forward and kiss her.

"You wanted to dance with me?"

She lowered her head, giving him a glimpse of her thick, brown lashes before looking up once more, training her jeweled orbs at him. "I…"

"Camille!" called Lady Collins. "You must come. The musicians have taken their seats."

Chapter Fourteen

The day of Miss Vane's picnic dawned sunny with a cloudless sky, promising once again to be unseasonably warm. Camille climbed out of bed and stood at the window in her bedchamber, studying a group of children playing on the grass with their governess looking on.

Once again, her thoughts strayed to Frederick. Their friendship had always been an untroubled, happy association. She had so many wonderful memories of dancing with him, sampling and offering each other their opinion of the newest flavors of ices at Gunter's, riding horses in the park, the laughter they shared after she beat him soundly in a game of shuttlecock at her brother's house party last summer.

A sense of dread hung over her as she ruminated on their current, awkward situation. All aspects of the relationship turned disconcerting when she informed Frederick of her plans to accompany her mother to Bath. His sudden barrage of questions had made her uncomfortable, causing her to inquire what he meant by his constraining manner. In that moment, he had been compelled to speak arbitrarily of his intentions.

This conclusion forced her to deliberate more deeply. In what manner, in any circumstances, could his declaration have been acceptable to her? Once again, she considered his words on that portentous day. She realized something quite important hadn't been spoken of. To what degree were Frederick's emotions involved? There had not been one word from him indicating his affection or love for her. Perhaps he saw their union as an amenable collaboration between two friends, allowing him the freedom to continue living his life without any profound changes or adjustments.

A knock sounded upon the door.

Camille turned to grab her wrapper from the back of a nearby chair. She shoved her arms inside the sleeves. "Come in."

"Good morning, Miss Collins." Sally walked inside the room balancing a tray. "I brought your hot chocolate and some toast."

"May I join you?" Ellen stood on the threshold, already dressed in a light pink morning gown, holding a cup and saucer in one hand.

"Of course. Sit down." Camille indicated the love seat in front of the fireplace. "Thank you, Sally. Please return in a few minutes to help me dress."

"Yes, miss." The maid curtsied to them and left.

Ellen settled herself on the love seat. "We were quite busy shopping with your mother yesterday and you retired early. There was no chance to speak to you alone. Something has been bothering me. I wished to inquire, did you find it surprising Lord Surd asked me to dance the minuet on Monday evening?"

Camille picked up a piece of toast, not looking at her. "Surprising? No, why should that be a remarkable occurrence?"

Ellen chuckled. "Don't be a goose, Camille! Whenever we attend a ball, Lord Surd makes a point to dance with you. He rarely seeks me out."

Camille determined never to admit to Ellen she had told Frederick she didn't want to dance with him. It would certainly cause bothersome scrutiny over her actions. She shrugged her shoulders, pretending disinterest. "Perhaps he planned to ask me to step out on the floor with him later in the evening."

Ellen set her cup and saucer down on the table. "But he was gone when I returned with Miss Warwick and Miss Talbot."

She took a bite of the toast and dropped the remainder onto her plate, before picking up her cup of chocolate. "Yes. He informed Mother and me that he had promised to leave the ball early in order to keep his uncle company. Apparently, his gout is causing him great discomfort."

Ellen frowned. "I was told by Miss Talbot he was suddenly called away with an urgent summons. Are you saying Lord Surd purposely avoided dancing with you and made up the excuse to leave?"

Camille choked on her beverage and paused to clear her throat. "N…No! That is not what I am implying at all! Why would you take anything Miss Talbot said as ingenuous? I am certain she fabricated the compelling request because she couldn't imagine anyone leaving a ball without having the great pleasure of dancing with her first."

Ellen picked up her cup and took a sip from it. "Very well. You are correct. I shouldn't have taken her conclusion as an incontestable circumstance. However, the fact remains Lord Surd did not ask you to dance the minuet when he had the chance and turned to me instead."

"I believe you are tormenting yourself over naught.

Lord Surd is under no obligation to dance with me at every ball we find ourselves attending together."

"I do not claim there is a requirement or a prior arrangement for Lord Surd to dance with you, Camille. Rather, I would say, on many occasions, he has demonstrated a decided preference."

"You pointed out a few days ago, Lord Surd is captivated by Mrs. Hervey," she reminded her. "Perhaps he was less than eager to participate in the dancing because she wasn't there."

Ellen's fingers tightened around her teacup. "He would never dance with Mrs. Hervey publicly at the Assembly Rooms if they had come to a formal agreement."

Camille took a deep breath as a searing pain pulled at the lining of her stomach. An image of Mrs. Hervey and Frederick deep in discussion on the outdoor terrace flickered before her eyes. "Do you believe they have come to an understanding?"

"There is a likelihood." Ellen pursed her lips together as she studied her. "I am quite sorry I ever mentioned the possibility, Camille. I never intended to cause you anxiety and distress."

A knock sounded upon the door before it was thrust open. Lady Collins strode inside the room. Sally followed behind her. "Good morning, ladies! You both should come downstairs and have something substantial to eat. We leave for Miss Vane's picnic in a couple of hours."

****

Frederick stared up at the ceiling while his valet shaved off his morning bristle. He had purposely avoided deliberating about the awkward situation with Camille yesterday, choosing instead to spend the day with his uncle. He accompanied him to have a soak in the King's Spa, noticing for the first time that a portion of the pools could be seen from the windows in the Pump Room. Thankfully, the area at the foot of the stairs, where Camille had misconstrued the ladies' spa entrance, was tucked away from view under a low-hanging ceiling. After a few minutes in the heated mineral water, they changed into their street clothes and emerged into the warm sunshine feeling vigorous and hungry. He walked behind the chairmen carrying his uncle to Sally Lunn's, a few blocks away. Frederick settled him into a seat near the door and propped his foot up on a crate. They proceeded to enjoy some of the delicious warm buns, served with butter, and washed down with cups of strong tea. From there, they stepped outside and flagged down another chair. His uncle informed him he would return to the townhouse but asked Frederick to stop by a bookseller on Milsom Street to purchase a particular volume on Repton's gardens he wished to study before joining him back at their lodging. They spent a quiet afternoon and evening together, reading books and newssheets from London. The day was topped off with a game of chess after dining on roast goose, boiled potatoes, and green beans.

As Frederick studied the early morning play of light and shadows on the beams overhead, he pondered the hasty conversation he had with Camille on Monday evening. She apologized to him in a roundabout fashion, mentioning her unfortunate tendency to speak tactlessly without due consideration to possible anxiety or hurt to others and her vow to moderate the lamentable tendency. In his view, she was exaggerating the amount of harm her frank mannerisms caused. He relished their conversations together. She had a talent for quickly determining a weak component in discussions on a variety of topics. He observed Camille and her brother Edward on several occasions participating in spirited arguments, but nothing was said that was purposely malicious or distressing. Rather, he usually sensed a grudging appreciation combined with a jot of frustration, on the part of both brother and sister, that they were unable to best the other after their spout of verbal jousting was concluded. And, as he pointed out to Camille earlier, he had also brought discomfort to Mrs. Hervey when he artlessly inquired after her husband.

He recalled the conversation he had with Mrs. Hervey and the methods used while being courted by her imminent husband. She admitted to being initially attracted by his appearance, but Captain Hervey's considerate, gracious behavior was what eventually won her heart.

Frederick knew there was absolutely no reason for Camille to believe he had behaved disrespectfully or thoughtlessly toward her. What had caused her to turn against him so suddenly? That was the impression her abrupt, incensed comment gave him. It felt as if they were no longer close friends, experiencing amusing, joyful moments, together in life as a devoted pair. Could she be uneasy, perhaps even terribly discomposed, by the thought of becoming his wife?

Certainly, Camille's refusal to dance with him was a new development. He always requested her partnership at balls they attended together. He would have previously thought she took as much pleasure in dancing with him as he did with her. Their relationship had always been full of carefree experiences providing him with abundant, pleasurable memories. He frowned. That was until he told her his intentions.

"Did I cut you, my lord?" his valet asked, as he stepped back, the blade clutched in his hand.

"No, no, Jasper. I had a momentary, disturbing thought. Carry on."

A short time later, after his valet had finished tying his cravat in a masterful knot and helped him into his coat, Frederick dismissed him. "I am going to attend a lecture this afternoon. I'm not certain when I will return."

"Very good, my lord." Jasper picked up the discarded pieces of clothing from the floor and quit the room.

Not yet ready to join his uncle for breakfast, Frederick strolled over to the window and stared down at the back alley. A local shopkeeper, with his cart full of goods passed by. He shooed a mangy cat lounging at the edge of the road away with a sweep of a large broom he held in his hand.

He took a deep breath, releasing the air slowly, as he suddenly recalled Camille standing close to Mr. Vane on Monday evening, her hand tightly gripping his forearm. Surely, it wasn't possible? She could not have accepted his proposal after such a brief acquaintance! Frederick tried to imagine experiencing life without Camille by his side as his wife. It was unthinkable. She was an integral part of him, a necessity. It was impossible to live without a beating heart, and just as hopeless for him to carry on happily without her.

He bent forward, resting his forehead against the cool glass. "Oh, Camille, what have I done?"

Chapter Fifteen

"Lady Collins! Miss Collins! Miss Cather! Welcome! Please, take a seat," called out Miss Vane as they walked across the grass toward her. She reclined in her push chair near the middle of a table that was covered with a white cloth, silverware, plates, and glasses. Her nurse stood behind her. "The others should arrive soon."

Lady Collins settled at a place opposite Miss Vane while Camille took a chair at the end of the table. Ellen sat down next to her.

"I am so happy the warm sunny days continue," Miss Vane gushed. "A picnic is never fun in cloudy, dismal weather."

"It is hard to recall a previous October that hasn't been cold and rainy," observed Lady Collins. "It is wonderful the exceptional climate has endured during our visit here."

"I see Mrs. Warwick and the others coming now." Ellen turned to face Miss Vane. "Is Mr. Vane going to join us?"

"Oh yes! My brother will be here shortly. He is inside organizing the servants as to who will carry out the beverages and who will oversee the food," she assured her. "Mrs. Warwick, Mr. and Miss Warwick, Miss Talbot, welcome!"

"Good day!" answered Mrs. Warwick. "Such a lovely afternoon for a picnic."

"It is exceedingly warm," pointed out Miss Talbot in a sullen manner. The lower half of her face could just be seen from underneath a broad-rimmed bonnet. "It would be mortifying to receive a sunburn."

"Disgraceful!" tittered Miss Warwick, twirling her parasol over her bonneted head.

"Take a seat facing away from the sun," advised Mrs. Warwick. "Keep your shawls draped over your arms, as well."

They settled themselves at the opposite end of the table and Mrs. Warwick took a place next to Lady Collins.

Mr. Warwick sauntered up to a seat across from Miss Talbot. "I intend to keep cool by drinking several pints of ale."

"I would advise you to wait until we see what beverages are offered before you announce your intentions," his sister cautioned.

"There will be an assortment to choose from," promised Miss Vane. "Here comes my brother now."

Mr. Vane strode up to the table with two footmen carrying trays following behind him. "I apologize for the delay. I have ale, cider, lemonade, sherry, or claret. The food will be transported outside shortly."

Everyone had their selection of beverage quickly seen to, and full glasses were placed in front of them. Two chamber maids appeared carrying baskets stuffed with a variety of fruits, cheeses, and bread. After placing a basket at either end of the table, they each bobbed a curtsey and turned back to the house. At the door, a portly gentleman wearing white gloves appeared holding a stack of plates on top of a folded serviette. The maids immediately halted their forward progress to allow the man to pass.

"Baldwin, distribute a dish to each of our guests," Mr. Vane ordered his butler. "No need to stand on ceremony. This is an informal event. Please help yourselves."

Miss Vane twisted around in her chair. "Miss Simms, sit down and have something to eat."

The nurse shook her head. "I will wait until you are served, Miss."

The footmen reappeared. One carried a joint of cold roast beef that had been thinly sliced. The other servant lugged a large, round dish covered with a golden crust.

"My cook's special dish, onion pie," Mr. Vane informed them. "If anyone wishes to sit on the grass after you have finished eating, Baldwin has brought out a few blankets for your use."

"This is lovely!" exclaimed Mrs. Warwick. "Your staff is quite efficient. Did you bring them with you?"

Mr. Vane took a seat at the table across from Camille. "Yes, I did. I find it is worth the extra expense to bring one's own servants from home. It leads to a smoother transition upon reaching the intended destination."

Miss Warwick and Miss Talbot sat with their bonneted heads close together. Between giggles and whispered comments, their gloved hands reached out for pieces of fruit and wedges of cheese. Mr. Warwick secured a pitcher of ale for himself. He gulped down the frothy liquid between copious mouthfuls of bread and roast beef.

"What would you like to eat, Miss Vane?" asked her nurse, as her charge sipped lemonade.

"I will have some fruit and a piece of bread," she

replied. "I want to let everyone know there will be plum cake and tea provided later."

"The onion pie is delicious," Ellen remarked. She put her fork down on her plate and patted her mouth with a serviette. "The crust is light and flaky, and the onions are quite tender."

"It is a favorite dish of mine," acknowledged Mr. Vane. He took a bite of fruit and looked up at Camille. "You are very quiet, Miss Collins."

She hastily swallowed a piece of cheese before addressing him. "I find the warm sun makes me drowsy."

"We had a busy day shopping yesterday as well," observed her mother. "My daughter and Miss Cather found several exquisite things."

"I am quite pleased to hear your outing was so successful," remarked Mrs. Warwick, with a smile. "Miss Cather, what items did you purchase?"

Ellen turned to her, enthusiastically describing the pieces she secured, with Lady Collins adding additional commentary.

"I wished to speak to you," Mr. Vane leaned forward, addressing Camille in a muffled voice. "My sister and I return to Tavistock next week. I dare not be away from the mine for any longer. I wished to invite you to travel with us, Lady Collins, and Miss Cather, as well."

Camille was surprised by his statement. She studied his perpetually brooding expression. The downturned, full-lipped mouth, his deep-set brown eyes that seemed to continually gaze at his surroundings in a gloomy, despondent manner. "I…We are honored to receive your invitation, however…"

"Before you decline, let me say that I wish to show

127

you my home. I will have my housekeeper give you a thorough tour. It would be best to familiarize yourself with the area as well. You should comprehend the true size of the city. The number of shopkeepers and type of wares available are of important consideration."

She experienced an anxious, nauseating wrench in her stomach as she thought she deduced the significance of his words. "I…"

"Miss Collins, I understand you purchased one of Mrs. Veazy's lovely bonnets yesterday. She carries the finest items. Did you obtain one of the hats decorated with French satin?" asked Mrs. Warwick.

"Yes, yes, I did," replied Camille, forcing the words out of her mouth as a deep sense of dismay engulfed her. Surely Mr. Vane could not be considering asking for her hand in marriage? She ruminated over her recent discussions with him, certain she hadn't given him the least sign of encouragement. "I found a straw bonnet with a broad rim lined with emerald-green satin, trimmed with translucent peach lace and pink roses."

"It sounds delightful, and the green will certainly bring out the unique color of your eyes," enthused Mrs. Warwick. "We must arrange an occasion for you to wear it. I have a suggestion. If the weather continues fine, I would like to propose an outing on Friday. Has anyone heard of Farleigh Castle?"

"Oh, Mother, that is a capital idea!" Miss Warwick stood up from her seat and clapped her hands together.

"Jolly good notion," agreed Mr. Warwick. A lusty belch escaped from his mouth, and he held his serviette up to his face. "Pardon."

"Is this castle a great distance from Bath?" asked Miss Vane, as she glanced at her brother. "If not, perhaps

I may be allowed to come as well."

"No, no. It is approximately eight miles from here," Mrs. Warwick clarified. "A well-sprung carriage should have no problem making the journey in an hour."

"Two or three carriages are required if all of us go," pointed out Mr. Vane. "We would need to transport your chair as well, Julianna."

"Farleigh Castle," repeated Ellen, with a far-away look in her eyes. "I believe the book I purchased a few days ago on the history of Bath has a section on the ruins there. I would love to see it!"

"Are any of the original castle buildings still standing?" asked Camille.

"Only the rock outlines and low walls of the Inner Court, Great Hall, kitchens, and bakehouse remain. Parts of two of the four towers yet endure," Mrs. Warwick informed her.

Camille sighed with satisfaction. The opportunity to explore a historical castle would provide a much-needed distraction from the other disconcerting issues she faced. "I am always interested in old relics and ancient remains."

"You will discover much to appreciate," Miss Warwick acknowledged. "The Priest's House is still intact as is the chapel of Saint Leonard. If you are not squeamish, you must visit the crypts below the North Chapel, which contains the tombs."

"Crypts and tombs?" murmured Miss Talbot, with a shudder.

"Oh, yes!" Miss Warwick affirmed, with a chuckle, obviously relishing her cousin's discomfort. "There are eight human-shaped lead coffins in the crypt. Some are adorned with ghoulish death masks."

Miss Talbot put her gloved hands over her ears. "Please stop! You are quite aware of my tender sensibilities!"

"Enough of your provoking mannerisms, Honora," admonished her mother. "I promise you, Priscilla, the two tombs in the family chapel are quite exceptional. They feature marble effigies of Sir Edward Hungerford III and his wife, Lady Margaret. They both passed away in the seventeenth century. There is also beautiful paintwork on the walls, some lovely stained glass, and wrought-iron railings forged in medieval times."

"Harcourt, could we please join in the expedition?" pleaded Miss Vane. "The ruins sound quite delightful!"

"No doubt the lurid descriptions of the chapel's interior appeal to your excessively overblown gothic tendencies?" her brother observed with a scowl. "I will need to ascertain if there is proper access for your chair. Mrs. Warwick, do you recall if the walkways surrounding the castle are paved or well-rolled? Are the inclines steep or gentle?"

"Carriages discharge passengers quite close to the main entrance, at the eastern gatehouse," she informed him. "There is a flat, paved walkway from the gatehouse leading to the chapel. The Inner Court is not level, being comprised of only remains of stone walls and foundations. As I mentioned, parts of two of the castle's towers still exist. Although it would not be possible to maneuver the push chair directly in front of them, your sister could easily view their remains from a level spot in front of the chapel."

Miss Vane clapped her hands together several times. "It sounds ideal! Please, Brother, may we join them?"

Mr. Vane stood up from his seat and walked over to

stand next to his sister. "If you promise to rest at home tomorrow, we will join the expedition on Friday."

She reached out to clutch his hand. "I give you my word, I will do as you ask. Thank you, Harcourt!"

"Miss Collins, you expressed an interest in ancient items," commented Mrs. Warwick. "Are you aware of the building in Bath Street, near the Pump Room, containing antiquities collected from the city of Bath?"

"No, ma'am, I did not know of it." She leaned forward in her seat to better observe the lady. "What type of relics are there?"

"I have browsed the items only once and it was several years ago." She frowned. "I recall an ancient urn, some old coins and medals, bits and pieces of old pottery, a huge stone axe, and a sarcophagus."

"I'd be happy to escort you and Miss Cather," Mr. Warwick spoke out, with a lop-sided grin at her. "Been there several times myself. The urn contains human bones, and the sarcophagus holds a skeleton."

"Please stop!" Miss Talbot shrieked.

"Herbert! Have a care! You are deliberately disregarding your cousin's susceptibility," scolded his mother.

"We must invite Lord Surd to come with us to Farleigh Castle," said Miss Vane with an impish smile at her brother.

He chuckled. "Very well. I will ascertain his address."

"I believe you may discover his direction in the Masters of Ceremonies' books in the Pump Room," advised Mrs. Warwick.

"Thank you. I will check there and send round an invitation." He nodded to her before turning away and training an intent gaze on Camille. He took a step toward her.

She dropped the piece of bread she was holding onto her plate with shaking fingers, knowing she must find an excuse to leave the picnic. She couldn't allow him to press her for an answer to his request to accompany him to his home. She stood up. "The sun is quite warm. I cannot eat anymore. Would anyone care to join me to see the Bath Antiquities display?"

"I previously offered my escort. I will come." Mr. Warwick gulped down the last of the ale in his tankard, patting his stomach as he rose from his chair.

"I will accompany you as well," announced Ellen with a smile, as she came to her feet. "Thank you so much for the lovely picnic."

Miss Warwick declined to join them, declaring she had seen the relics several times already. Miss Talbot shivered and shook her head. Mrs. Warwick and Lady Collins announced their intention to stay and sit on one of the blankets in the shade of a large elm tree.

"I'm sorry you must leave, but it is quite sultry," remarked Miss Vane as she shook each of their hands. "You will miss Cook's delicious sponge cake."

"Are you certain you are well, Camille?" asked Lady Collins, with a frown. "You are flushed."

"Do not fret, Mother. It is extremely oppressive sitting in one spot. Walking will revive me." She turned to join the others, starting in surprise when she found Mr. Vane standing next to her.

"I realized I failed to inform you that we leave for Tavistock next Wednesday. If you have any further questions for me, I will gladly address them on Friday while we are exploring the castle. Also, I will need your brother's direction."

Chapter Sixteen

Frederick returned to his uncle's residence later that afternoon, after attending the discussion on the exploration of Egypt with Mrs. Hervey. He had managed to present himself at her doorstep just as she opened her door and stepped across the threshold. She was obviously surprised by his unplanned appearance but after he explained remembering her reference to the lecture on Wednesday afternoon and wishing to be present, she graciously accepted his escort.

Rigsby opened the door to him. "Good afternoon, my lord. I trust you enjoyed the lecture?"

"Yes, I did. But I must admit I have no intention to join in any upcoming exhibition. I much prefer to allow the experts in the field to hold sway. To hear about having picnics on top of pyramids, riding camels instead of horses and discovering ancient tombs is all quite enthralling. However, I admit I am partial to exploring the lands of my own country. Hearty British food and a clean, comfortable bed at the end of a day of adventure will do quite well for me!"

"Most definitely, my lord!" The butler held out a silver plate containing a folded missive. "This came for you an hour ago."

"Thank you." He picked up the note, studying his name and uncle's direction written in unrecognizable, scrawling handwriting before breaking the seal.

Lord Surd,

As we continue to be graced with fine weather, Mrs. Warwick proposed an outing to Farleigh Castle on Friday. The ruin is said to be a mere eight miles away and features several ancient coffins (some displaying death masks), tucked away in a crypt underneath the family chapel.

Everyone attending our picnic today expressed great interest in joining the excursion. My sister asked that I extend an invitation to you. (If Mr. Melter is feeling up to the trip, please bestow a request for him to join us as well.)

I understand Mrs. Warwick does not own a carriage. My coach will hold myself, Julianna, her nurse, and perhaps one or two other occupants. Lady Collins' vehicle will convey several more. If you and your uncle agree to come with us, I would be obliged if you would bring your own carriage.

I propose we leave the city by eleven o'clock, with the intention of arriving at the castle around noon. I will have my cook put together a basket of modest provisions, such as ale, lemonade, bread, and cheese.

Harcourt Vane

Frederick's first thought after he read the note, was how pleasant it would be to get away from the confines of the city for a few hours. "Rigsby, where is my uncle?"

"He is in the drawing room, my lord."

"Very good." He strode up the stairs, down the corridor, past the stairs leading to the bedchambers and opened the door to the drawing room. He checked his stride on the threshold. "Uncle! You are standing on your own two feet!"

He grinned at him. "Can you believe it? I woke up

this morning to discover the swelling had gone, and the tingling pains have disappeared."

"Wonderful! Do you have a notion of what brought on the sudden improvement?"

"The surgeon stopped by to have a look at me. He believes a combination of a healthier diet, no port, and the mineral baths have done the trick." He walked across the room and sat in a chair by the window. "I have been advised to go slowly."

Frederick took the chair facing him. "I agree. It would be a shame to exhaust yourself after making such wonderful progress."

He turned away to gaze out of the window. "I admit this fine weather makes me long to ride a horse again."

Frederick held up the note. "I have a proposition. I received an invitation from Mr. Vane, to join him and several others on Friday for a trip to Farleigh Castle. Are you familiar with it?"

His uncle raised his brows. "No, I can't say I am."

"He informs me the castle is an easy one-hour trip. I visited the stables yesterday, where my cattle and carriage are being looked after. My coachman mentioned the horses could do with some good exercise. An outing of this nature would certainly provide it."

"I sent my vehicle back to my estate," his uncle remarked. "We would need to use your carriage. Other than Mr. Vane, who would be joining us?"

"His sister, Miss Vane, Miss Vane's nurse, Lady Collins, Miss Collins, Miss Cather, Mrs. Warwick, accompanied by her son and daughter, and Miss Talbot." Frederick counted off the names with his fingers.

"We will require three carriages then."

"Correct. If you wish to go, I will write Mr. Vane an

acceptance and offer to take up Mr. and Miss Warwick in my vehicle. Miss Talbot could ride in the Vane coach."

"Quite a group of friends you seem to have acquired in a short period of time, Frederick!" His uncle chuckled.

"One of the ladies is an acquaintance of long-standing," he clarified, with a smile.

****

Camille stabbed her needle haphazardly into her embroidery as she glanced at her mother and Ellen, both sitting across from her on the sofa, intently reading their books. A few minutes more, and then she would excuse herself and retreat to the privacy of her bedchamber.

"I believe I will go to my room and finish the chapter there," announced Ellen, closing her book and standing up. "I had a lovely day. I will see you both in the morning."

Camille bounded out of her chair, tossing her embroidery to the floor. "I believe I will go up as well."

"Stay, Daughter." Her mother gave her a piercing stare. "I wish to speak to you. Good night, Ellen."

"Good night."

The door closed behind her. Camille faced her mother. "What is it you want to talk to me about?"

"Sit down, please." She shut her book with a quick, snapping motion, and placed it next to her on the sofa, never once looking away from Camille. "I have noticed the constraint between you and Lord Surd. I am confused by it, and I wish for an explanation to its cause."

"There is nothing wrong, Mother."

"Camille! Cease this prevarication!" She glared at her. "Lord Surd has been a frequent attendant and friend to you since he came to your rescue over five years ago.

He graciously escorted us both to visit your injured brother last year and accompanied us on our return to Horsham House. It was obvious to me he had developed deep feelings for you. What has happened?"

"Oh Mother!" Camille sobbed as her knees gave way and she sank back down on the chair. "It is all such a muddle!"

She reached across and handed her a handkerchief. "Explain, please."

Camille hastily wiped the scrap of material across her eyes. "Before we left, I unexpectedly came upon Fre...Lord Surd. He mentioned he was surprised to find me in London. I told him our arrangement to travel to Bath in a few days' time. I also informed him of Edward's sudden marriage to Sophia, explaining our intention to visit your friend in Bath in order to give the newly wedded couple their privacy."

"I imagine the news of Edward's marriage took him by surprise?"

"Oh yes! In fact, I believe that is where the confusion began." Camille paused, pressing her lips together as she vividly recalled that day. "You see, he told me he intended to visit Edward to ask for his permission to pay his addresses to me."

"I knew it!" Mother smiled widely and then frowned. "Why have you both adopted this restrained, timid manner when you are together? Surely there is no issue if Lord Surd is required to wait a few weeks to confront Edward with his request?"

"When he informed me of his intentions..." The tears formed at the corners of her eyes, and she dabbed at the wet trails on her cheeks with the handkerchief. "I was astounded and confused. I had never contemplated our relationship. He was always there when I needed him. I thought of him only as a stalwart, dependable friend."

Her mother nodded her head. "I can easily comprehend how you reached that conclusion. Lord Surd came into your life when you were a young girl. His quick thinking and expeditious actions saved you from serious injury. Your father had passed away the year before. Perhaps unconsciously, you began thinking of Lord Surd as your champion or defender. A resolute, constant friend in the sincerest manner."

"Precisely, Mother! Which is why I informed him, while I was honored to know of his intended offer, I was not ready to get married. I told Lord Surd there were many other things I wanted to accomplish first."

"Oh, Camille!" Lady Collins compressed her lips together as she glanced up at the ceiling, taking several deep breaths, before turning to glare at her. "I have frequently bemoaned the fact that you tend to be an outspoken, head-strong young lady, but you are also quite intelligent, and until now, used those discerning traits to come about nicely with little harm done. Never have I been so disappointed in you!"

"But Mother, Lord Surd's proposal was completely unexpected!"

"I understand, Camille. However, I find it hard to believe you were completely ignorant of the strong emotions I know you hold for him."

She sighed and twisted the handkerchief between her fingers. "I have always been indebted to him for coming to my rescue when I was fourteen. There have been numerous times when I have thanked him for his escort to parties and balls. We were both grateful to him for accompanying us on the journey to Berkshire to check on Edward after he was injured."

"I am not referring to your feelings of appreciation or sense of obligation to Lord Surd. Of course, the fact that he saved you from suffering a grievous injury is something we could never reciprocate or ever express adequate gratification for. I was referring to the affinity you both have toward one another when you are together. I have observed a unique rapport and comprehension between the two of you. There is no doubt in my mind you care deeply for him."

"Of course I do, Mother! But how am I to know his feelings? Does he wish to marry me because I am a loyal friend? Am I to simply be his comfortable companion and helpmate?"

Her brows rose and she sat up straight against the back of her chair. "Did Lord Surd fail to inform you how he felt?"

"He did not mention his sentiments! There was no opportunity. He certainly was not prepared to speak of his intentions at that moment. You could say I forced his hand. I was astonished and bewildered by the knowledge he meant to court me and uttered the first thing that came to mind."

"Which was effectively a negative answer," Lady Collins pointed out. "What a predicament! This misunderstanding needs to be resolved as soon as possible. We must create an opportunity for both of you to have a serious discussion together. Perhaps he will attend the Fancy Ball tomorrow evening."

A knock sounded upon the door. Bowles walked inside the room and bowed. He held out a silver salver with a folded piece of paper on it. "I have just received a missive addressed to you, Lady Collins."

She held out her hand. "Thank you, Bowles. You may go. I will let you know if there is a reply."

"Very good, Lady Collins." He bowed again and went back out to the corridor, closing the door behind him.

She opened the folded paper and scanned the message. "It is from Ruth. Apparently, Lord Surd and his uncle will be joining us on Friday for the excursion to Farleigh Castle. He has invited Mr. and Miss Warwick to join them in his carriage. Mr. Vane will take Miss Talbot in addition to Miss Vane and her nurse. Ruth asks if she may join the three of us in our vehicle."

Camille was preoccupied with disordered musings on how she would go about extricating herself from the confusion she had created. She replied in a perfunctory manner. "Very well."

Lady Collins gazed intently at the carpet as she tapped her cheek with one finger. "I intend to change the plans, Camille. This is our chance to put you and Lord Surd together in a confined space. While certainly not private, it may provide you with an opportunity to explain to him why you reacted in the way you did."

"How do you intend to accomplish that, Mother?"

"I will simply inform Lord Surd that you and Ellen will ride with him instead and tell Ruth that Herbert and Honora will ride with us in my carriage."

"Won't Lord Surd feel you are being presumptuous?"

Lady Collins chuckled. "When you are my age, you will discover most people will overlook the bothersome characteristic of self-assertion. It is considered one of the many foibles of the elderly."

"Oh, Mother! I doubt Lord Surd considers you to be so very ancient."

"Perhaps not. In any case, his manners are too affable to complain about the change. It is my belief he will welcome the adjustment."

Camille frowned. "I must determine how best to explain the situation without sounding arrogant."

"Use the time wisely, my dear."

"Yes, Mother." She came to her feet. "I will go to bed now."

"Stay a moment." Lady Collins stood up and reached into a concealed pocket on her skirt and pulled out a sealed piece of parchment. "Edward sent a letter to me. He enclosed this for you."

She reached for the note. "Thank you, Mother. Good night."

Upon reaching her bedchamber, Camille quickly stepped inside and closed the door behind her. She strode over to the sofa and sat down, pulling at the seal, and opening the missive.

Camille,

I imagine it was quite a shock to learn Sophia and I are married. You are one of her close friends, and along with many others, you believed her to be an uncaring, self-centered individual. You would be wrong. I will not provide you with personal details that are Sophia's alone to provide to you, but I want to make you aware, my wife hid her true, compassionate, kindhearted nature from others.

I want to caution you, little sister, using the lessons I learned in my relationship with Sophia. Never take someone for granted you care about. I could have easily ignored the sense something was not right when Sophia allowed the armor that she carried about her person slip when I was injured. It would have been a simple matter to believe she had made a temporary lapse in judgement. She was sequestered in her aunt's home in the country, away from the distraction of societies' entertainments. She was bored, looking for a temporary way to amuse herself.

But I knew, deep in my soul, she was the woman I had been searching for to complete myself. Using my heightened sense of connection to her, I guessed some of her story and eventually impelled her to reveal her true self to me.

Now I am happier than I ever thought I could be. I have a beautiful, loving companion who will be by my side for the rest of my days.

Never risk the loss of someone dear to you, Camille. Show them how important they are to you. Take a stand, push forward, persevere, demonstrate to them how much you care. You will never forgive yourself if you lose them.

Edward

"Oh!" It was a shock to know Sophia had been presenting a false demeanor to her for so long. More dismaying were Edward's cautionary statements. Her hand shook and the note slipped from her fingers, fluttering to the floor. She squeezed her eyes shut as an unwieldy, constricting pain began inside her chest, as if a lump of bread dough pressed against her lungs. She coughed, forcing out short, rapid gulps of air before slumping backward against the sofa cushion.

As her breathing settled into a moderately regular pattern, she concentrated on every aspect of the quandary she had created, and recognized Edward was correct. She would never forgive herself if Frederick turned away from her and she forever lost his regard. She desperately needed to make him understand how much she loved him. But how was she to go about doing so? It would never do for her to arrive on his doorstep asking to speak to him with no maid in attendance. And what of the precarious situation with Mrs. Hervey?

Chapter Seventeen

Frederick accompanied his uncle to the spa on Thursday, returning to the townhouse in the early afternoon without venturing out again in the evening. He decided to forego attending the Fancy Ball. To be present at that event would only make the situation with Camille more uncomfortable if she were there. He hoped for a chance to speak with her while on the Farleigh Castle excursion.

He had been advised that the other occupants of his carriage would meet him and his uncle in front of the stables on Bennett Street at ten in the morning on Friday. His coachman had just finished attaching the traces and the shafts to the horses. Frederick watched as the animals were led outside.

"I trust we haven't kept you waiting, Lord Surd!"

He twisted around, hastily bowing. "Miss Cather, Miss Collins?"

Camille's soft cheeks turned rosy as she peered at him from underneath the rim of her bonnet. "I hope you do not mind if we join you. Plans were changed with little notice. Mrs. Warwick believed it would simplify matters if her son and daughter rode with her and Mother."

"I have no objections to the transition. I greatly appreciate having both of you accompany us on this adventure! Please, come meet my uncle." He led them around to the other side of the carriage where he was conversing with his coachman. "I would like to introduce Miss Collins and Miss Cather. Ladies, this is my uncle, Mr. Melter."

He bowed to them and then thrust his arm out to clasp each of their gloved hands in turn. "Charmed, Miss Collins, Miss Cather! The anticipation I had for the journey ahead has increased substantially, knowing we will have such lovely ladies as companions!"

Frederick pondered the actual reason for the adjustment in travel arrangements. It occurred to him, it would have been much easier for Lady Collins to bring her daughter and Miss Cather in her carriage. He would attempt to discover why the change was made later. While his uncle was conversing, he discreetly contemplated the ladies' attire. Miss Cather was looking quite handsome in a French grey, long-sleeved walking gown. The bottom of the skirt was decorated with white lutestring, edged with cord, the ends ornamented with small, white roses. She wore a straw-colored silk hat on her head. It had an oval crown. The brim was slightly turned upward into a soft roll on each side of her face.

Camille's round gown, in a light peach hue, was trimmed lengthwise at the bottom edge of the skirt with contrasting salmon-colored plaits. Her long sleeves were ornamented by rows of three satin rouleaux and finished at the edge with white crimped satin, scalloped at the ends. Her bonnet featured a round crown, lined with emerald-green material, finished at the edges by a deep fall of translucent peach colored lace and several tiny, pink roses. A matching wide band tied underneath her chin.

His coachman climbed into his seat, taking the reins,

while a stable boy let down the steps and opened the carriage door.

Frederick swept his arm out in front of him. "Ladies, please make yourselves comfortable."

Miss Cather stepped forward, placing her gloved hand in his. She smiled at him. "Thank you very much, Lord Surd."

Camille followed closely behind her, faltering when she hesitated for a moment, to avoid stepping on her friend's skirt. "Oh!"

Frederick quickly reached out, wrapping his arm around her waist. "No harm done. I've got you!"

She looked up at him with a wobbly smile. "Thank you for saving me once again!"

He bent over to whisper in her ear. "I will expect to collect my reward at a more appropriate time."

He heard her catch her breath, but she made no reply, moving toward the carriage door and taking the stable boy's hand as he helped her inside.

"Uncle? Take your time going up."

He slowly climbed the steps, pausing at the top to study the interior of the carriage. "What is this? Surely you ladies have had enough of each other's company. One of you, please sit next to me and delight me with tales of the amusements and activities you have participated in since you came to the city."

Miss Cather stood up, laughing as she moved to the opposite seat. "Certainly, Mr. Melter!"

"Capital!" His uncle lowered himself next to her onto the smooth leather upholstery.

Frederick strode up the steps, taking the spot next to Camille. The door shut behind him and the carriage surged forward.

"Where are we to meet the rest of our party?" asked his uncle, as he leaned back against the seat.

"We are to join the other two carriages on Lansdown Road. I understand that is the most direct route to the castle." Frederick glanced out of the window. "I see Mr. Vane now. He is signaling to my coachman and climbing back into his vehicle. Lady Collins' coach is waiting just behind. We are on our way."

"Are you familiar with the castle we are to visit, Miss Cather?" His uncle inquired.

"As a matter of fact, I purchased a volume on the architecture of Bath and the surrounding area shortly after we arrived. I brought the book with me." She pointed to the rectangular-shaped lump protruding from her reticule. "I was quite excited to discover a chapter in it on Farleigh Castle. Miss Collins and I had a chance to look over the pages yesterday."

"Please, describe to me anything you might have noted of interest."

As Miss Cather regaled his uncle with her findings, Frederick turned to Camille. He was surprised to find her staring at him. "What is it?"

"My mother orchestrated this. I wished to tell you how sorry I am that we did not dance together at the Dress Ball on Monday evening," she murmured.

"You cannot be more regretful than I am," he replied, bending down to softly speak the words into her ear, relishing the enticing scent of lemon coming from the dark brown ringlets clustered against her cheek. "I am confused. I thought you did not want to dance with me."

She flushed as she glanced toward the others and tugged on the crown of her bonnet so that one side of her face was partially concealed. "I previously made an effort to explain the situation to you. Recall, you were my very first partner at my coming-out ball, a truly momentous occasion I will always remember. Please know this, it will always be one of my greatest desires to dance with you. Ignore me if I ever claim otherwise again."

He chuckled as he stared at her glorious emerald, green eyes. "You understand you have placed me in a precarious position with your request?"

Her thin, dark brown brows lowered as she studied him. "How so?"

He sighed. "I have given you my promise not to make a nuisance of myself by frequently seeking your company while we are both visiting Bath. How am I to keep my vow and be present at every ball you attend while in the city? I must disregard your appeal."

Her eyes widened and a puff of air emerged from her parted, sweetly curved red lips. "I understand."

"It would never do for Miss Talbot to know such a thing occurred at the castle! Don't you agree, Camille?" Miss Cather's voice rang out in the carriage.

Camille moved away from him, sitting back against the seat. "What are you referring to, Ellen?"

"I was telling Mr. Melter the story we read about Agnes Cotell, the lady who strangled her husband with his own handkerchief in the kitchen of the castle," she reiterated.

"Oh!" She chuckled. "No! She must never know a murder took place there."

"Does Miss Talbot have what is commonly known as *tender sensibilities*?" Frederick asked.

Miss Cather giggled. "She used those very words to

characterize her flaw. Miss Warwick described to us the interior of the castle chapel at the picnic on Wednesday. When she mentioned crypts and ghoulish death masks, Miss Talbot nearly swooned!"

"The anticipation I have to visit this ruin is rapidly building," remarked Mr. Melter, rubbing his gloved hands together. "Did Agnes happen to be the castle cook?"

"Her husband was the steward to Sir Edward Hungerford in 1518. Sir Edward was a descendant of the original owners. Sir Thomas Hungerford built the castle in the late thirteen hundreds," Camille clarified. "Shortly after John Cotell was killed, Agnes became Lady Hungerford."

"Quite an outrageous and diabolical woman," observed his uncle.

"I am afraid her nefariousness did not stop at strangulation. With the help of two yeomen from Wiltshire, his body was lifted inside the castle oven and incinerated," Miss Cather added.

"The woman's utter brazenness is quite disturbing," Frederick remarked, with a frown. "I trust she was tried and sentenced for her appalling deed?"

"Eventually, yes. Whether her second husband was involved in the murder, it is unclear, but while he was alive, Lady Hungerford was protected," Camille explained. "When Sir Edward died in 1522, proceedings were quickly started against her and her accomplices for the murder of her first husband. She was convicted and hanged at Tyburn in February of 1523."

"A just and fitting end for such an evil woman." His uncle turned back to Miss Cather. "You were speaking of death masks. I know a likeness was created of

Napoleon at his death. I imagine they are similar?"

"Yes, I believe so. I read there are eight human-shaped coffins dating from the seventeenth century in the crypt beneath the north chapel. The coffins are made of lead…"

Camille gripped Frederick's hand as she leaned over to whisper, "We will be attending the Fancy Ball on Tuesday evening in the lower rooms. I give you leave to disregard your previous vow to me. Please come."

****

Their carriage followed the other two past what appeared to be a gatehouse. After traveling several more yards, the coachmen pulled the horses to a stop in the middle of an open, flat field. Several other coaches were already parked nearby.

Frederick offered his hand to Camille and Ellen as they exited the carriage before carefully assisting his uncle. He had confessed to experiencing some pain in his leg just prior to reaching their destination.

Camille sighed as she studied the two partially standing towers on the other side of the stone wall surrounding the clearing where the carriages were parked. Other than raising his brows at her earlier request to join them at the ball Tuesday evening, Frederick had not responded to her entreaty.

"Miss Collins! We are going to make our way to the chapel first. Would you care to join us?" called out Miss Vane from her chair, as her nurse tucked a blanket over her legs and lap. Her brother stood at the back of the chair, staring at her with hooded eyes and the typical somber, ruminating expression on his face.

Camille glanced over at the others. Frederick was busy seeing to his uncle. Ellen had joined Miss Talbot,

Miss Warwick, and her brother. She was caught up in listing the various curiosities she wished to view while pointing to the chapter relating to the castle in her book. Her mother and Mrs. Warwick were strolling down a smooth, dirt walkway toward what looked like the remains of a central courtyard and the castle ruins.

"Thank you. I will gladly come with you."

They made their way down the path and through the gatehouse entrance. An old man, with the butt of a clay pipe hanging to one side of his mouth, stepped out from a small room tucked away behind a stone wall. He held a piece of parchment in his hand. "Welcome to Farleigh Castle. This here is a rough drawing of the property. We are standing in the outer court. The inner court is in front of us. You will be able to see low walls and outlines of the Great Hall, the kitchens, bakehouse, and moat. The foundations of two of the towers also remain. Of special interest is the southeast tower, also known as the Lady Tower. You can observe the remnants of the original five floors and parts of the circular staircase there. Still intact is the Chapel of Saint Leonard, just to the right. Please follow the path to the entrance. Be certain to visit the small north chapel added under Lady Joan Hungerford's direction in the 1400's. We also have the Priest's House behind the chapel. That is not open to the public."

Miss Vane took the map from him. "Thank you, sir."

They made their way toward the chapel with Mr. Vane easily pushing the chair across the smooth, graveled walkway.

"I wonder why the one tower is referred to as the Lady Tower?" he commented, with a frown.

"It is a sad tale. Miss Cather and I were reading about the castle last night," Camille informed them.

"Apparently, Lady Elizabeth Hungerford, the wife of Sir Walter Hungerford III, was imprisoned in the tower by her husband. She was forced to drink her own urine and eat meager scraps of food, secretly supplied to her by local women, for over three years before she was finally released upon the arrest of her husband."

"How horrible for Lady Elizabeth!" exclaimed Miss Vane. "I hope her husband was duly punished for his terrible exploits?"

"He had become a patron of Thomas Cromwell. Sir Walter's association with him proved to be his downfall. He was charged with treason and executed with Thomas Cromwell in 1540."

"A fitting end for such an evil man." Miss Vane consulted the map. "Apparently, there are four marble effigies inside the chapel as well as the eight lead coffins down below in the crypt."

"The entrance to the chapel is just ahead," remarked Mr. Vane, as he pushed the chair around a pile of rocks and up to the doorway. "It appears the floor is covered in centuries-old stone rubbed smooth by people walking across it for hundreds of years. Go ahead of us, Miss Collins, Miss Sims."

Camille entered the chapel and her gaze was immediately captured by the stained-glass window at the rear of the room. To the left of the window, there seemed to be another small enclosure, framed by a grouping of roughly carved, iron railings. She took a few more steps forward, peering at the figures inside the iron cage.

"I believe these represent Sir Thomas Hungerford and his second wife Lady Joan." Miss Vane studied the paper as her brother pushed her into the room. "Sir Thomas built the castle. It was completed in 1383. He died fifteen years later. Lady Joan passed away in 1412."

"The other two effigies are here." Camille pointed to two intricately carved figures lying side by side on the other side of the room. Their heads rested on hard marble pillows decorated with sculpted embroidery and tassels. "I suppose this is Sir Edward Hungerford III and his wife Lady Margaret. She ordered this separate chapel built after the death of her husband in 1648."

"Notice the carving at his feet?" asked Mr. Vane, as he positioned the chair a few inches away. "I believe that is a heraldic badge of some sort."

Miss Vane considered the map once again. "You are correct, Harcourt. Lady Margaret was a Peverell before her marriage. The badge represents the union of the Hungerford sickles and the Peverell wheatsheaf."

"Quite interesting." Camille walked to the other side of the effigies to study a large chest. It was crudely painted in a rose-pink color with dark green accents. There were fluted pilasters around the edge, with a shield at the center. She pointed to it. "I think this is the Hungerford family shield."

"Yes. It is called a tomb-chest." Mr. Vane took the parchment from his sister's hand and studied it. "Sir Walter's remains are inside. He left this earth in 1596."

"Where is the entrance to the crypt, Harcourt?" Miss Vane gripped her gloved hands together as she stared at him with glowing eyes.

"Unable to contain your delight in all things ghoulish, eh, Julianna?" her brother teased. "I'm sorry, my dear, but I doubt I will be able to maneuver your chair down the stairs."

"If the opening leading down to the crypt is wide enough, I would be happy to assist you with the chair," called Lord Surd from the other side of the room.

"Oh! Yes! Thank you, my lord, for offering your assistance." Miss Vane turned in her chair and gave him a warm smile.

"We must determine if such a thing is possible first, Julianna," cautioned her brother.

The doorway to the crypt was discovered just outside the main chapel entrance. It was quickly established that the steps were wide and stable enough to allow the men and the chair to safely descend. Camille entered the chamber first. Miss Sims chose to wait outside, her handkerchief clutched in her hand, while the men carried Miss Vane down to the crypt.

The eight human-shaped coffins were lined up along the walls of a small, damp, and musty cavern. Two of the coffins were tiny, infant-sized, and four of the remaining ones had molded, adult faces on them.

As she studied the various expressions on the death masks, Camille put out her hand and gripped the side of Miss Vane's chair.

"Had enough of this fiendish, revolting atmosphere, Miss Collins?" asked Mr. Vane, with a sinister twist to his mouth.

"Yes. I am quite ready to leave." She took a faltering, jittery breath and felt a touch on her arm. She turned to discover Frederick standing close by. He was studying her with intense concentration.

"Go on up ahead of us. I will be directly behind you."

Camille gulped mouthfuls of the fresh, clean air as she reached the top of the stairs and stepped outside. She saw that her mother, Ellen, the Warwick family, and Miss Talbot had joined the fretful nurse as she waited nervously for her charge's return. Mr. Melter sat on a rustic bench a few feet away.

"Are you feeling better?" Frederick stared down at her as he placed his hand on her forearm.

"Yes. Thank you." She took another deep breath. "The atmosphere inside the crypt was quite stifling."

"If you are certain. I must go back and help remove Miss Vane."

Her lips quivered as she smiled at him. "I am much better now that I am outside."

A few minutes later, the two men appeared in the doorway, carrying Miss Vane wedged in her chair between them.

A lusty cheer emerged from Mr. Warwick's mouth. "We believed you had been carried away by a crazed specter!"

Mr. Vane frowned at him and then announced that some refreshments, consisting of ale, lemonade, bread, and cheese had been spread out on blankets in the grassy area underneath the trees, near where the coaches were parked. They all made their way over to the food and drink.

Camille sat in a group with her mother, Mrs. Warwick, and Ellen. She gratefully sipped the sweet, tangy lemonade, and nibbled on chunks of bread and cheese while she listened to the others discuss what they had seen on their tour.

"I could barely breathe when I saw the death masks!" Miss Talbot clutched at the ribbons from her bonnet, tied securely underneath her chin. "It is a wonder I didn't collapse in an untidy heap on the floor!"

The sweet sound of birdsong broke over Miss Talbot's chattering voice. Camille was suddenly consumed by a frantic need to be alone. She came to her feet, her hands haphazardly brushing her skirts. Without informing the others of her design, she made her way past the low walls and the remains of the inner courts' foundations, to the surrounding woods. She strolled under the tall elm trees, their large limbs moving gently in the light breeze, and took a deep breath. The tight muscles in her back and neck loosened. She closed her eyes and sighed, grateful for the momentary sense of contentment.

"Miss Collins! There has been no opportunity for us to speak about my plans for departure next week. Will you and your party be joining us?"

Camille slowly turned toward Mr. Vane, conscious of the feelings of strained apprehension rapidly returning. This awkward situation must be dealt with. "I am sorry. You have not been comprehensible with me. What are your intentions?"

His thick black brows rose, and his shrouded eyes suddenly opened widely, allowing her to see into the depths of his dark brown orbs. "Didn't I make myself clear? I wish for you to become my wife."

She took a deep breath. "There was no mention of that. You simply invited me, Mother, and Miss Cather to accompany you and your sister on your return to Tavistock. Although it was implied, you made no reference to marriage."

He groaned, tugging at his neckcloth. "I apologize! I warned you previously, I am lacking in refinement and discipline when it comes to wooing ladies."

"It will not be necessary for you to further clarify this matter. Mr. Vane, while I am honored to be considered by you for the role of your wife, I am sorry, I cannot accept your offer."

"Camille! Where are you?"

She gazed past Mr. Vane's shoulder at Frederick striding through the undergrowth, forgetting to conceal the desire and longing reflected in her eyes.

"I see. I apologize. I did not comprehend…" Mr. Vane cleared his throat and bowed to her, before straightening up and walking away.

"I trust everything was resolved to your satisfaction?" Frederick's expression was grim. His jaw clenched.

She smiled, reaching out to him with trembling hands. "Yes. I am so re…"

He backed away from her. "We must depart. My uncle's leg is paining him."

Chapter Eighteen

Upon their return from Farleigh Castle, Frederick had been intent on making his uncle as comfortable as possible. After overseeing his safe removal from the carriage into a chair, he took his leave of Camille and Miss Cather and requested a groom from the stables to escort them back to their residence. Once the ladies had walked away, offering their thanks and well wishes to his uncle, he closely followed the Bath chair back to their residence.

Rigsby's concern clearly showed on his face when he opened the door at Frederick's knock and observed his master clutching his leg and grimacing. "Sir! What has happened?"

Frederick supported his uncle as he moved to get out of the chair. "Please send a note round to Mr. Melter's surgeon and ask him to come as quickly as possible."

From that moment until late last night, all Frederick's attention had been concentrated on his uncle, making certain the pain in his leg lessened. Grimsby, with the help of Jasper, had quickly removed his boots and clothing, before putting him in a clean nightshirt and laying him on his bed with his sore leg elevated by several pillows. The surgeon arrived moments later. After examining his affected limb, he massaged the leg, using quick even strokes and kneading motions with his hands. After several minutes of watching helplessly as his uncle grunted and groaned with each manipulation, Frederick couldn't keep silent any longer.

"Are you certain this is helping him?"

The surgeon stopped the rotating motions and gently placed his uncle's limb back onto the pillows. "Gout is caused by reduced blood flow brought about by excessive salts in the system, my lord. Mr. Melter has made great improvements by changing his diet. He overextended himself today. The massage will stimulate and augment the circulation. With rest and minimal walking, he should notice a significant improvement in twenty-four hours."

"Is there anything I can do in the meantime?"

The surgeon wiped his hands on a towel and reached for his bag. "Make certain he stays off his feet for the most part, continues to eat the foods I have prescribed, and drinks a full pitcher of water. I will return to check him tomorrow afternoon."

When the bedchamber door closed behind the surgeon, Frederick turned to his uncle. "I am quite sorry I suggested the outing to Farleigh Castle today, sir. I hate to see you in such pain."

He took the handkerchief Grimsby offered him and wiped the sweat from his brow. "Do not blame yourself for my discomfort, Frederick. I was eager to go. Clearly, I pushed myself too far, too fast. The pressure is less intense after the massage. I will try to sleep. Come check on me tomorrow."

When Frederick entered his uncle's bedchamber late Saturday morning, he was surprised to discover him out of his bed, sitting in a chair, reading the latest newssheets from London. A pitcher of water and a goblet were on a table nearby.

"Uncle! You are feeling better?"

He lowered the paper and smiled at him. "I'm much improved, Frederick! I was able to sleep most of the night. The surgeon stopped by an hour ago and gave me another massage. He advised me to stay home and rest for the next two days. If the pain and discomfort continue to abate, he gave me permission to visit the Pump Room on Monday afternoon."

"The Pump Room?" Frederick grinned, the sense of considerable satisfaction at his uncle's rapid improvement making him feel lightheaded. "Do you intend to try the waters once more to determine if your initial impression was incorrect?"

"Not at all! It is unlikely my opinion will ever alter on the viability of drinking Bath water. Rather, it was my design to attempt to gain an introduction to an amicable, mature woman. You have had no problem procuring new acquaintances in the short time you have been here."

"Indeed! I wish you much luck with your endeavor. In the meantime, I will stay home and keep you company."

Though his uncle had initially protested, Frederick quickly made him understand that he was determined to share his temporary confinement. They spent the time reading, discussing current reforms up for debate in Parliament and the tragedy of the Peterloo Massacre in Manchester. The day came to a satisfactory end after playing several rounds of chess.

Upon visiting his uncle's bedchamber the next morning, Frederick found him awake, strolling around his room wearing slippers and a red satin dressing gown over his night shirt. "Uncle! I am quite pleased to see you up and walking."

"I have made substantial progress." He smiled. "I intend to rest again so I will be in top form for our visit to the Pump Room tomorrow."

"I will gladly keep you company today."

"There is no need. I am perfectly fine on my own. Join me for dinner if you will."

"Certainly!" Frederick watched him as he walked across the room to sit on the sofa with no outward sign of discomfort. "Very well. I believe I will attend the twelve o'clock church service at the Bath Abbey. I'm told the music produced from the organ is exceptionally fine."

"Jolly good notion! The stained glass and fan vaulted ceilings are remarkable as well."

"I will see you later then." He exited his uncle's room, making his way down the passage to his bedchamber. His valet was there, folding shirts in the connecting dressing room.

"Jasper, I am attending the services at the Abbey this afternoon. I will need my black double-breasted, cutaway frock coat and the black breeches. I will try out my new boots as well."

"Very good, my lord." He quickly obtained the requested garments.

After he donned the various articles of clothing, with his valet's assistance, Frederick glanced in the dressing room's mirror. His servant had managed to outfit him in a record amount of time. Jasper moved behind him, adjusting and smoothing the material on his coat.

His valet stepped away. "All finished, my lord."

"Thank you." He reached for his hat and gloves. "I don't plan to be away too long. I believe Mr. Melter means to rest in his rooms most of the day."

"I understand, my lord."

Frederick strode out of his bedchamber, quickly walking down the stairs to the front entry, eager to be outdoors again. He intended to stop at Mrs. Hervey's home and offer his escort to the church. He made his way down Lansdown Road to Broad Street and turned down Green Street. As he approached Quiet Street, he heard women's voices, raised in exasperation.

"Something must be done, Beatrice! The door won't close properly!"

"We can't force it to lie flat, ma'am."

Frederick turned the corner and saw Mrs. Hervey standing on the top step leading to the entrance of her townhouse. Her housekeeper was visible inside the house, behind the partially open door. "Mrs. Hervey! May I be of assistance?"

She swiveled around to face him, her face flushed. She wore a muslin gown ornamented in a silk leaf pattern, a straw bonnet with a spray of tiny silk flowers on the brim covered her head and a matching reticule with gold filagree straps was draped over one arm. "Lord Surd! I wish you might help. The floorboard in the entry has become loose. It is warped and rubbing against the bottom of the door. I am afraid to force it shut, thinking the wood on the floor will become scratched and the door will no longer open."

He frowned. "You mentioned someone living with you who took care of repairs?"

She sighed, clutching her reticule with shaking hands. "Yes. My cook's husband. Unfortunately, I gave Mr. and Mrs. Longman the day off. They are visiting their daughter and her family in a village several miles from here. I don't expect them back until evening."

Frederick addressed the housekeeper. "Do you happen to know where Mr. Longman keeps his hammer and nails? I will secure the board until your man returns and can fix it properly."

She studied him without speaking for several seconds. "I believe I do, my lord. I will be a moment."

"I apologize, Lord Surd." Mrs. Hervey pursed her lips. "I spoke out of turn. I never expected you to do this."

He smiled at her, before removing his hat and pulling off his gloves. "There is no obligation to express remorse. I have determined a simple way to compensate me for this trifling service to you."

"How am I to repay you?"

He dropped his gloves into his hat and handed it to her. "You may begin by holding my hat, gloves, and coat for me. After I complete my task, I hope you will allow me to escort you to the Abbey."

"Gladly."

He shrugged his arms out of the sleeves of his coat and handed the garment to her. "Thank you, ma'am."

"Here is the hammer and some nails, my lord," called out the housekeeper from the doorway.

"Excellent." He took the items from her and bent over to push the warped board flat upon the floor. Holding it down with the pad of his left hand, he took one of the loose nails and placed the tip against the wood, gripping it with his forefinger and thumb. He clutched the hammer handle with his right hand and pounded the nail into the edge of the floorboard, securing it in place. He stood up and pushed the door completely open, handing the tool and remaining nails to the housekeeper. "That should do for the present."

"Wonderful! Thank you so much, my lord." Mrs. Hervey sighed and gave him a warm smile.

"Thank you, Lord Surd," murmured the other lady. "I will see you later, ma'am."

The door closed behind her. Frederick took his coat from Mrs. Hervey. He heard a tinkling of ladies' voices and glanced at the street. Camille and Miss Cather walked into his line of vision moments later. He quickly shoved his arms into the sleeves of his coat. "Good morning!"

"Good day!" called Mrs. Hervey.

"Lord Surd, Mrs. Hervey!" Miss Cather called out, before glancing at Camille.

"G…Good day," she faltered and looked away.

Miss Cather cleared her throat. "I'm sorry. We cannot stop. We promised to meet Lady Collins in front of the Abbey some time ago."

"Carry on!" Frederick frowned as Mrs. Hervey handed him his hat and gloves. The sight of Camille had reminded him once more of the appalling possibility that she had accepted a proposal from Mr. Vane. "We will certainly see you there."

"I trust nothing has occurred to cause a difficulty in your relationship with Miss Collins?" Mrs. Hervey remarked as she placed her hand on his forearm and they walked toward New Bond Street.

He raised his brows and studied her expression. "Is my regard for her so apparent?"

"Not at all," she assured him. "Pardon me. It was my conjecture, after you questioned me about my courtship with Thomas, claiming you wished to give advice to *a friend*, you were most likely seeking the counsel for yourself. Perhaps I am unduly watchful, but I detected a unique affinity between the two of you that first day in the Pump Room. I am distressed to perceive an undercurrent of strain and apprehension now."

He sighed. "You are correct. Recent events have conspired to create mistrust and unease between us, where previously we had a warm, delightful relationship with complete confidence in one another. I confess I am at a loss how to regain that special bond."

They turned onto High Street. The Bath Abbey tower rose majestically in the sky directly in front of them.

"I wish to recommend a course of action to you," Mrs. Hervey murmured as she suddenly came to a stop. "You must have a serious discussion with Miss Collins. I have a suspicion there have been misunderstandings that have caused needless confusion and worry."

He grimaced. "That is all very well...one moment! Is it possible for you to visit the Pump Room tomorrow afternoon, around one o'clock? I made plans to escort my uncle there. Would you consent to keep him company while I ask Lady Collins for permission to have a private conversation with her daughter?"

Chapter Nineteen

Camille sat next to Ellen on the sofa in the drawing room, pretending to read the book on the history of Bath during the seventeenth century that she had borrowed from the circulating library the week before. Her mother, accompanied by her maid, had gone to meet Mrs. Warwick at the Pump Room. As Camille stared down at the pages, tears swam in her eyes. The words and pictures were nothing more than a hazy blur.

Frederick was truly lost to her. The sight of him standing in front of Mrs. Hervey's residence yesterday without his coat on, provided Camille with clear evidence she could no longer ignore. He had come to an agreement with the widow, whether for a temporary liaison or something more permanent, it mattered not. It would be impossible for her to accept such an arrangement as his wife. The sense of pain and great loss was overwhelming. Without his familiar presence in her daily life, she couldn't imagine how she would go on. He was as essential to her as a door on a house, a root on a tree, or a wing on a bird. She sniffed and wiped at her face with the back of one hand. Contrary, recalcitrant woman! She received her just deserts for her wayward, stubborn attitude. He had been on the point of offering for her and she had balked, spouting some nonsense to him about needing more time to experience the world on her own terms. Too late, she had comprehended that without Frederick at her side, the universe was nothing more than a bleak, empty shell.

A knock suddenly sounded on the door, and it opened. Bowles stood on the threshold. "A Miss Talbot and Mr. Warwick are asking if either of you are at home."

"Yes. Please show them in." Camille stood up, dropping the book on the seat, as she reached into her pocket for her handkerchief.

"Are you well?" Ellen got up from the sofa and walked toward her, never taking her intent gaze off her face.

"Yes." Camille wiped at the moisture clinging to the tips of her eyelashes.

Ellen frowned. "Are you certain? You skirted my queries this morning. I thought I heard odd noises coming from your bedchamber last night. Were you crying? Is there anything I can do for you?"

Camille pursed her lips, looking away. She was disconcerted to know her wretched disposition last evening had been exposed. "I'm sorry I disturbed you. We will speak later."

"Miss Talbot and Mr. Warwick!" announced Bowles from the door.

The two of them entered the room in their typical, boisterous manner. Miss Talbot flounced in first with Mr. Warwick swaggering behind her.

"Lovely to see you both, Miss Collins, and Miss Cather!" blurted Miss Talbot as she swung her parasol back and forth in her gloved hand, narrowly missing a porcelain figurine on a nearby table.

"Good day," murmured Camille. "Will you have some tea?"

"No, no." Mr. Warwick nudged his cousin to one side and stepped forward, his portly belly straining against the buttons on his bottle-green waistcoat. "We had the brilliant notion to take a stroll in Sydney Gardens and afterward, partake of some refreshments there. We were wondering if you ladies would care to join us?"

"I am sorry, I cannot go," Ellen informed them, before turning to Camille. "Recall I am otherwise engaged. I agreed to accompany Mrs. and Miss Warwick on a shopping excursion later today."

"Oh, yes. I had forgotten. Silly me," Miss Talbot simpered. "Honora mentioned the engagement this morning. No matter. Do say you will come with us, Miss Collins. It is quite warm outside. I am eager for an adventure and the gardens are just the place to indulge in one."

"Indeed. There is certainly much opportunity for such a contingency," preened Mr. Warwick. "The garden contains a grotto, a loggia, as well as a temple. Although I have attempted it only once several years ago, an especially enterprising endeavor would be to enter the labyrinth and venture to find Merlin's Swings and Hermit Cave at the center."

"I do not think…"

"I believe you should go," Ellen interrupted Camille's intended refusal. "A change of scene will do you good. It sounds as if there will be plenty of diversions to draw your attention away from other matters."

Camille turned away to look out of the window. The sun was shining, and the limbs of the large elm trees emerging from the grassy fringe across the road, were scarcely moving in the gentle breeze. Perhaps she should distract herself from her maudlin thoughts. There was no advantage to sitting by herself wiping at her tears for the duration of the day. She swung around to face the others. "Very well. Allow me to change my gown and put on my walking shoes."

A few minutes later, she emerged from the townhouse with Miss Talbot and Mr. Warwick following behind.

"There is no sense staying indoors on such a lovely day," pointed out Miss Talbot, as she unfurled her parasol, leading the way down Brock Street.

"There will be reparation soon. I predict, within a fortnight, we will have snow," Mr. Warwick announced with a snicker as he sauntered down the street.

Miss Talbot stopped her forward progress and glared at him. "How churlish you are, Cousin! Why must you speak of this? Is it your intention to check and stifle our enjoyment of the day?"

"Not at all! I am merely reminding you of Britain's renowned, changeable weather." He projected his chin outward in a superior manner.

"Whatever your ulterior motives may be, I wish to amuse myself. I have a matter I wish to speak of with Miss Collins. You may follow us at your leisure." With this bold statement, she wrapped her gloved hand around Camille's arm, leading her past The Circus and down Gay Street. "It is my understanding Mr. and Miss Vane intend to depart on Wednesday. I imagine you will experience great affliction from Mr. Vane's absence."

Camille turned away from her contemplation of two greyhounds, diligently followed by a footman. Both dogs were pulling and straining on their leads, obviously eager to reach open space where they could stretch their long legs. "I do not comprehend your statement. Why should I react so intensely once Mr. Vane has returned to his home?"

Miss Talbot twirled her parasol over her bonneted head, staring at Camille with half-closed eyes, while she adopted a sly, knowing expression. "I observed your earnest discussion while strolling with him the other day in the woodland bordering Farleigh Castle. Surely you cannot blame me for assuming your affections were engaged?"

Camille's extremely sensitive emotional state did not allow for careful consideration of her words. "I do admonish you most severely! Never, ever, make suppositions upon whom I give my devotion to."

Miss Talbot's eyes widened, no doubt in shock at Camille's bitter response. "I am sorry!"

"Look alive, ladies!" called out Mr. Warwick. "Here is Bridge Street. Once we cross Great Pulteney Street, the park will be a few steps away. We must purchase tickets at the tavern first."

Camille looked away from Miss Talbot's stricken expression, to discover they were quite close to the River Avon. She turned back to her companion. "Please understand, you are alluding to a sensitive, personal concern. I will not have my private life bandied about in such a callous, dissembling manner. Rather, I would be indebted to you, Miss Talbot, if you could manage to divert my thoughts away from the profound melancholy that has possessed me for most of my time in Bath. Shall we do our best to enjoy the gardens?"

****

Frederick stepped forward as the attendants carrying the Bath chair his uncle was riding in, pulled up in front of the Pump Room. One of the men opened the door on the contraption. "How was the ride down the hill, sir?"

He climbed out of the chair, pulling on the sleeves of his coat. "Quite smooth. No harm done."

"Capital! Shall we make our way inside?"

"Lord Surd!"

He turned to see Mrs. Hervey making her way past a group of elderly gentlemen and a flower seller. "Good day! Come and meet my uncle. This is my friend Mrs. Hervey. Mrs. Hervey, my uncle Mr. Melter."

"I…I can't believe it! You found her!"

"Pardon?"

She smiled at Frederick, a rosy blush spreading across her cheeks. "I thought you reminded me of someone. The yellow, golden hue is a unique hair color."

"Can you find it in your heart to forgive me, Mrs. Hervey? I acted such a fool!" His uncle bowed low over her outstretched hand.

She chuckled. "You were a young man, intent on experiencing London in the same frenzied manner of a myriad of impetuous gentlemen over the decades."

"You can't mean…?" Frederick gazed intently at them.

"Yes! This is the lady I told you about." His uncle turned and looked over his shoulder. "Your husband does not accompany you, Mrs. Hervey?"

Her smile dimmed. "I am a widow, Mr. Melter. My husband died in the Battle of Waterloo."

"I apologize! I now recall my nephew mentioned something of that nature."

"Please, may we go inside and converse?" She glanced at Frederick. "I believe Lord Surd has a task to complete. Will you keep me company for a short period,

Mr. Melter?"

"Of course, I will! Run along, nephew!"

"Very well. Enjoy yourselves!" He grinned and shook his head as he turned away, silently acknowledging the providential chance that brought the two of them together once more.

Frederick crossed the street, quickly making his way up Union Street to New Bond and Milsom Streets. Then across George and Gay Streets, past The Circus to Brock Street, finally to the Royal Crescent. He strode up the front steps of the townhouse and banged on the door with his fist. It was swiftly opened by a dour-faced butler. "I need to speak to Lady Collins immediately. Inform her Lord Surd is making the request."

The man swung the portal open wide. "Come in, my lord. Follow me."

He trailed the butler halfway down a long corridor, where he abruptly came to a stop in front of a door, embellished by a gleaming, golden knob. He knocked against the hard surface before twisting the knob and striding inside. "Lord Surd to see you, Lady Collins, on a matter of some urgency."

Frederick stepped forward into the room and bowed. "Lady Collins. I must ask your permission to have a discussion with your daughter alone. I require only a few minutes of her time."

She stood up from a chair set close to the hearth, dropped an open book on the seat, and walked toward him. "Lord Surd. I am sorry. Camille left over an hour ago to stroll through Sydney Gardens with Mr. Warwick and Miss Talbot."

"Thank you. I will see if I can encounter her there."

She put out her hand to clutch his arm. "Is something

wrong?"

"No. No. A misunderstanding, that is all. I bid you a good day." He patted her hand and turned away, sprinting out of the room and down the corridor to the front entry.

"My lord." The butler bowed and opened the door.

He dashed down the stairs to the street.

"Lord Surd! Wait! It is imperative I speak to you."

He swung around and saw Miss Cather crossing the road, swiftly making her way toward him. Frustrated at the delay, he took a deep breath and exhaled before uttering, "What is it?"

"There is something I must tell you." Her trembling fingers twisted and pulled the handkerchief she held in one hand. "I made a comment several days ago. I was surmising a probable situation. I fear my conjecture has given a false interpretation. I heard Camille sobbing in her bedchamber last night. I tried to talk to her. She rebuffed my queries at breakfast this morning. I believe I could be responsible for her anguish."

Alarmed by the image of Camille crying alone in her room, he resisted the sudden urge to reach out and shake Miss Cather, only by bracing his arms against his side. "Tell me!"

"The day you and Mrs. Hervey had tea together on the terrace outside the Lower Rooms, Camille and I walked past and spotted you both. I inquired if we should present ourselves, but Camille declined, saying she believed you wouldn't welcome our company." She wiped at a tear as it fell from the corner of one eye.

"Go on."

"I...I mentioned you appeared quite enchanted with the lady and gave my view that this development was not surprising."

His heart pounded in an agitated, tumultuous cadence. He stiffened his stance and glared at her, his fingers clutched tightly together inside his gloves. "You presume to be familiar with my deeper emotions?"

Her face flushed a crimson red. "No, no! It was an assumption. Camille challenged my comment. I reminded her…the gossips say that young gentlemen often use lonely widows to further their experience before marriage."

"How could you have the audacity to say such things to her?" Frederick clenched his teeth together admonishing himself not to say anymore. He pivoted away, surging down across the grassy bank, toward Sydney Gardens, knowing the current mortifying state of his relationship with Camille had to be rectified without delay.

Chapter Twenty

Camille trudged along the pathway inside the labyrinth in Sydney Gardens while she searched the area in front of her, looking for a familiar landmark or recognizable rock or tree that they would have passed as they made their way to the center of the maze.

"We have taken the wrong turn! Bother the old swing!" Miss Talbot groaned. "I shall never be able to return in time for tea!"

Camille took a deep breath and sighed heavily. Mr. Warwick and Miss Talbot had been discussing what they planned to wear to the Fancy Ball tomorrow evening ever since they had entered the labyrinth. She wasn't surprised they had no notion of how to retrace their steps to the entrance. She turned to face the others. "I suppose we should have taken the other trail we came upon near the waterfall. I thought we traversed the one on the left when we entered. It appears I was wrong."

"I thought I made myself clear, Miss Collins," Mr. Warwick growled between gritted teeth. He stepped toward her, his arms stretched outward, his fingers curled inward like claws. "You were to remember which path we took to get in so we could easily find our way out."

"I believed we came this way." To excuse his threatening stance and harsh words, Camille acknowledged to herself they were all tired and discouraged. But an image of her shoulders bloodied and bruised from his powerful, constricting grip caused her to step back off the trail. Her right foot slipped into a hole. It was clamped tightly within the damp soil. A horrifying mental picture of slithering snakes inside the soft earth caused her to yank her leg. A throbbing pain reverberated across her foot. "Oh!"

"We are accomplishing nothing by standing here arguing," Miss Talbot grumbled, ignoring her exclamation, as she thrust the tip of her parasol into the ground.

Camille took one step forward and immediately reached out to grasp a nearby tree trunk as a burning contraction gripped her foot. She sighed in weary exasperation and swatted at the tears that were forming at the corners of her eyes. "I…I have twisted my ankle. You must both fashion a type of sling with your arms and carry me out of the labyrinth."

"Quite an unfortunate occurrence for you, Miss Collins. However, you have failed to consider all aspects of your request." Mr. Warwick extended one foot, contemplating his shining, black leather pumps with a worshipful gaze. "Your notion has no chance of success. The process of carrying you would be extremely awkward. There is a good possibility we would drop you. I have a better thought. Miss Talbot and I could easily make our way back to the entrance. We will summon a servant to come assist you."

"Only…Only moments ago, you claimed we were lost."

"I have had a chance to reflect on the matter. Finding our way out simply requires a process of elimination," he clarified. "I believe you are correct when you stated a wrong course was chosen. We will return to the waterfall. It shouldn't be too difficult to find our way to the entrance from there. Someone will be sent to aid you. Come, Miss Talbot."

"But…" With a speed Camille hadn't known either of her sulking companions possessed, they strode away, vanishing behind the thick, green shrubs bordering the path. Gripping the tree, she put all her weight on her unharmed limb, and studied her surroundings. Partially concealed by a large, flowering bush, she could make out a bench tucked away off the trail on the other side of the path. She slowly made her way toward it, hopping on one foot, pausing to take occasional deep breaths while keeping her injured leg raised up off the ground.

Several agonizing minutes later, she finally reached the secluded seat and lowered herself onto the hard, wooden slats with a sigh. Remembering something about the need to elevate a limb after suffering an injury like hers, she twisted around on the bench, intending to lift her leg and recline across the seat.

"Camille! Where are you?"

"Frederick! I am here. On the bench on the other side of the yellow flowering bush." Her heartbeat surged at the sound of his deep voice, and she gulped down a sob that threatened to emerge from her throat. Moments later, he stood before her.

He lowered himself to squat down on his heels in front of her, gazing intently at her face. "I came upon the others. They told me what occurred. Are you in pain?"

She leaned forward, studying him with an eager anticipation, not unlike a lost, thirsty traveler in the middle of a desert who had just spotted a mirage. "My ankle is quite sore. I cannot walk. How will I ever get out of here?"

"I have a plan." He took her gloved hand in his, giving it a light squeeze. "I am sorry I took so long to find you. Mr. Warwick's directions could be described as imperfect at best."

She gave him a wobbly smile. "I am quite happy you are here. I know I can trust you to think of the best solution to the unfortunate quandary I find myself in."

"Will you allow me to inspect your ankle? If there is swelling, I must remove your shoe before any further damage is done."

"Oh, yes. Of course. It is my right foot." She grasped a swath of fabric on the front of her gown, lifting the material up over her slipper.

"Your ankle is swollen. I will be as gentle as possible." He stripped off one of his gloves, carefully reaching for her foot.

"Oh!" A heady warmth infused her body as his bare fingers lightly brushed her ankle.

He stopped moving and looked at her. "Did I hurt you?"

"No…No! Please continue. Ah!" She tipped her head back, looking up at the canopy of tree limbs overhead as Frederick removed her shoe and some of the intense pressure went away. "It feels much better."

"I am gratified to hear that." He came to his feet, stuffing her slipper inside his coat pocket before putting on his glove once more. "A surgeon needs to examine your injury as soon as possible. We must make our way out of here."

"How will we manage?"

"I intend to carry you."

"No! Frederick…Lord Surd, I am much too heavy!"

"Back to formalities again, are we?" He grinned at

her and bent over, placing one hand at her back and the other under her legs. He lifted her up, holding her tightly against his broad chest. "I rather enjoyed hearing my first name upon your lips."

She ducked her head beneath his jutting chin as a wave of heat coursed across her face, breathing in the enticing scent of sandalwood, when the end of his cravat tickled her nose. "You surely cannot intend to carry me through the entire labyrinth! We had just left the hermit's cave at the center when I wrenched my ankle."

"Hermit's cave? You must describe his abode in detail to me while we make our way out to the entrance."

She huffed. "It was nothing out of the ordinary, I assure you. Merely a damp indentation in the side of a hill. If I had known it held so little interest, I would have declined to enter the labyrinth and I would never have suffered an injury. Though, I must admit Merlin's swing was entertaining."

"A swing as well? We must come back when your ankle has healed." He grinned down at her. "As much as I hate to see you in pain, I am enjoying the opportunity to carry you in my arms."

An unexpected impression came to her from many years ago of Frederick grasping the reins on her runaway horse and pulling the mare to a halt. "Oh!"

He came to an immediate stop. "Did I hurt you? Should I put you down?"

"No. No. I am well." A wailing sound escaped her mouth as the tears suddenly cascaded down across her face.

"Camille! What is wrong?" He gently lowered her to a sitting position on a nearby fallen log, making certain her injured ankle was protected. He sat beside her, reaching out to clutch her hands.

She hunched her shoulders, staring down at their clasped fingers. "I had an image of you stopping my mare all those years ago, most probably saving my life. You escorted me and Mother to Berkshire to check on my brother after he had his accident. Now I sprain my ankle and you come to my rescue. You must be heartily sick of me!"

He gently squeezed her hands. "Never! Camille, must I remind you of my wish to marry you?"

She turned away, mumbling, "It is not uncommon to make a request without first deliberating over all aspects and repercussions."

He didn't reply for several seconds. "Are you implying I am sorry for informing you I intended to ask your brother for his permission to pay my addresses to you?"

She faced him, looking directly into his warm, brown eyes. "It was an awkward moment. You didn't realize what you were saying. You required additional familiarity, understanding. I cannot live that way."

He pressed his lips together and sighed. "Is this a roundabout manner of telling me to go *further my experience* and forget about marrying you?"

"Well, yes. Yes, it is."

He let go of her hands and crossed his arms in front of his chest. "For the second time today, I want to shake some sense into Miss Cather."

"Ellen? What has she done?"

"She has put ideas in your charming head that have no business being there! Would it surprise you to hear that at this moment, Mrs. Hervey is in the Pump Room listening to my uncle describe how he fell in love with her at first sight at a ball in London more than twenty years ago?"

"Your uncle and Mrs. Hervey?"

He placed one hand on the log and leaned toward her. "Yes. You already know, Mrs. Hervey is a sweet, timid widow. I had the opportunity to save her from a couple of nasty mongrels on my first day in Bath." He frowned. "I admit, she served as a convenient companion after I promised to refrain from being continually at your side. We have spent much time discussing a variety of interesting topics. You are aware I attended a lecture with her as well as serving as her escort to the Abbey last Sunday after I performed a temporary repair on one of her floorboards. That is the entire underpinning of our acquaintance."

She fanned her flushed cheeks with one hand. "Is that why you were not wearing your coat?"

He glared at her. "Don't tell me you believed I had been up to something nefarious with her!"

"I was so perplexed!"

He turned away from her, taking a deep breath. "I am confused as well. Could it be possible? Please tell me I am wrong, Camille! Did you agree to become Mr. Vane's wife?"

She gasped. "No, never!"

He frowned at her. "I believed he asked for your hand when we were at Farleigh Castle."

"He did ask me there, in a roundabout fashion." She pursed her lips together, deliberating how best to explain. "He indicated that he wished for me, Mother, and Ellen to visit his home, he referenced a need for my brother's direction, but he never said the actual words. I was forced to ask him to clearly state his intentions."

"When I came upon you both in the woods, it was obvious a serious discussion was taking place. After Mr. Vane abruptly walked away, I enquired if the situation had been resolved. You appeared so happy."

She stared at him. "Yet another mix-up! At that moment, I experienced such a wondrous sense of relief and solace. Mr. Vane understood I had feelings for you and withdrew his request for me to become his wife."

Frederick cleared his throat. "You told him you cared for me?"

"I'm afraid I failed to hide the emotion I felt for you. I am certain it was reflected in my eyes when I saw you striding toward me." She looked away, embarrassed by her admission.

"You reassure me!" He chuckled and put a hand on her shoulder, turning her to face him. "I can think of one course of action to make the situation crystal clear."

She sat up straight, with her brows raised. "Here, Frederick?"

He ignored her query, gently wrapping his hand around the back of her neck, nudging her close to him. He placed his lips on hers, softly pecking and nuzzling her mouth.

She gasped at the warm, dizzying sensation quickly overtaking her entire body. The tip of Frederick's tongue entered her mouth, stroking her bottom lip. She marveled at the heady feeling, snuggling closer to him, and without conscious thought, mimicked his actions. Their tongues dueled together for several moments.

Frederick suddenly pulled away from her, his chest rising and falling as he took several gulps of air. He gazed at her for a moment and then grinned. "You seem to have disregarded your previous concern about the location?"

She giggled, reaching up to wrap her arms around his neck. "Indeed, I have. I am certain I will never again question the suitability of receiving a kiss from you."

"I will see you have no reason to, my dear." He smiled down at her before placing the pad of his gloved thumb against her face, gently stroking her temple. "I trust you are no longer bewildered about the strength of my feelings for you. I love you, Camille. You had my heart from the moment you gave me a dazzling smile, wrapped your arms around me, and kissed my cheek before blithely thanking me for saving you from falling off your horse!"

"As long as that? You shock me, Frederick!"

"You must agree, I have been quite patient." He reached inside the front panel of his coat, pulled out a small box tied with a green ribbon and handed it to her. "I carried this around with me for several days."

She took the box with shaking hands, yanked on the ribbon, and opened the box. "The turquoise brooch! It's lovely, Frederick!"

"Allow me." He picked up the trinket and fastened it to the front of her bodice. "The color is a compliment to your glorious green eyes. Do you recall the meaning, Camille?"

She giggled. "True love!"

He reached out to push a wayward curl off her cheek. "Lasting, true love, my dear!"

She took his hand in her own, gently squeezing it. "I pledge to you, Frederick, I shall love you forever and ever."

He placed a kiss on their entwined hands before coming to his feet. "We must get you back so you can have your ankle checked by the surgeon. I'm sorry, you will most probably have to forego the ball tomorrow evening."

Camille laughed as Frederick picked her up, holding her tightly against his chest. "As long as I am able to waltz with you at our wedding, I won't complain."

He chuckled. "I will make certain nothing occurs to confound your wish!"

Author's Note

It is a joy to write historical fiction because it allows me to combine real life elements with my own improvisations. I used the pamphlet entitled *Walks Through Bath* by Pierce Egan, printed for Meyler and son, 1819, to follow, as closely as possible, the facts about the city. Many of the shops and addresses are real, as are the names of the Masters of Ceremonies. The minuet was still danced in the Upper Rooms during this time period, but only one couple would usually preform the dance. When I discovered, from an authority on dances of the Regency period, that the steps of the minuet took up a fraction of space on a ballroom floor, I adjusted the dance to allow three couples to perform it at the same time.

Farleigh Hungerford Castle is an English Heritage site. I researched their website and studied various images for my description of the ruins.

A word about the author…

Cynthia Moore grew up in a small, southern California beach town. While many hours were spent lying on the sand, she always had a book in hand, or a paperback tucked inside a bag ready to pull out and read after a quick splash in the waves. Cynthia discovered British literature as a teenager. After reading most of the Victorian classics, she was introduced to English Regency period novels in 1987. It was love at first read. Since that time, Cynthia has read over four thousand fiction novels and owns a large collection of research books about the fascinating era. She is extremely proud to have several published stories set during the Regency and resides in Southern California with her dog who is, not surprisingly, named Austen. www.cynthiamooreauthor.com

Thank you for purchasing
this publication of The Wild Rose Press, Inc.

For questions or more information
contact us at
info@thewildrosepress.com.

The Wild Rose Press, Inc.
www.thewildrosepress.com